SHRIMP COPTALES

MICHAEL ANDERSEN

ISBN Softcover: 978-1-922821-99-7

DEDICATION
To the memories of Dad and Danny…
what memories they are!

WITH THANKS
To all who supported and encouraged my scribbles.
You know who you are.

My special thanks to Lesley for getting this collection together
between its covers.

WITH LOVE
My sweet, sweet Jemmie.
May God bless you as He has blessed me.

CONTENTS

PERFECTION

Why they called it the perfection knot, he did not know. He'd made his way, with great care, down the slope to the few square metres of accessible riverbank to forget the world and to concentrate on enjoying the natural bush, the lazy flowing river, and the possibility of catching three or four fish.

He was one of those people who seemed to get by without too much preparation in life. Even during his days as a detective, he attacked life as it was. Not that things fell into his lap, he knew the more work he put into something, the greater the success. His best fishing excursions were when he'd prepared everything before loading the car. His best success as a policeman of any rank came when he did his homework. But the best results weren't necessarily the most satisfying. In the old days, he always had a rod in the boot of his car and in his police car. Often on a case he would pull up by a bridge or along river track and try his luck. Many times his luck was in, not just with catching fish, but with catching his criminal quarry. Fishing had always given him the ability to allow solutions to come to him.

Today, though, he was just Shrimp. He never thought of himself as Dan, Danny, Daniel, Mr. Nolan or Detective Nolan. Just Shrimp. It was the nickname bestowed upon him when he was kid fishing muddy inland rivers. Shrimp was the only bait he would use. Later on, he would discover lures. The lure he selected this day was purple with a flash of red. Shrimp wondered if fish notice the colours on a lure. Somewhere in an angling magazine he had read that fish were not colour blind, so the colour selection must be important. Green worked well in the later part of the year. When there was a touch of tannin colour in the water, usually after a summer storm, bronze colours seemed to attract the fish. When they weren't interested, it didn't matter what colours were tried, they would not attack what was offered.

He could have had his lure tied, but the spontaneity of his decision to wet a line meant the fiddly things needed to be done when he reached the secluded stretch of river about thirty kilometres from home. His landing net was always within arm's length, a keeper net was tied to a log half submerged, and his clothes and hat sprayed with insect repellent. Not his hands. No repellent must touch the terminal tackle. That would put the fish off. He held the purple, shallow diving device gently between his lips by the bib as he worked the fluorocarbon leader, invisible to the fish once in the water, into the perfection knot to secure the lure whilst permitting it to "swim" naturally when being retrieved.

Satisfied, Shrimp worked the water. As always, the initial casts were cause for the most anticipation. After that, it became automatic, not mundane, but routine. It was a perfect morning. He might be lucky enough to hook onto a Murray cod. The cod was the perfect ambush predator. There was that word again. Perfect! The perfection knot, a perfect morning, the perfect predator. Perfect played on his mind like a tune he could remember but couldn't put a name to.

IAN BISHOP CLIMBED into his work ute. The paddocks were devoid of crops. He would not sow for somebody else to reap. His property had been on the market for only a relatively short time. Seasons had been good for the past four years and the place was in prime condition when he decided to sell. The agents had prospective buyers contacting them almost every day, looking for such a place, so it wasn't long before negotiations started.

Forty-one years is long enough, Bishop reasoned. Let someone of younger years, more enthusiasm and a full wallet ease his burden of gambling with the seasons. What stock he had he'd take to the sales where prices were good. He'd kill one fat steer to fill his freezer and keep him in meat for some time to come. The cattle were only a sideline. Cropping was what had kept him going.

With agents calling to show interested parties over the place, things were set in motion for a clearing sale. In these parts, a clearing sale would see genuine bidders and sticky-beaks alike. Not having married, all his energies were ploughed into the chocolate brown soils that stretched from dawn in the east to sunset in the west. His sheds were well maintained, surface water was the next best thing to permanent and, if needed, ground water could be tapped into with bores.

For a long time, many had waited for Bishop to hold a clearing sale at Gerry Downs. They knew whatever they were to bid on would be quality. Everything on Gerry Downs was top quality and in top working condition, from pliers to ploughs, from tin snips to tractors. They also knew that like the property itself, everything in the clearing sale would bring top dollar.

SHRIMP'S rod and reel rested against the trunk of a huge gumtree. He had been fishing for about an hour and a half. He had two fish in the keeper and had about four strikes without hook up and one fish had spat the lure as he manoeuvred the landing net to bring that fish to bank.

The distant hum of a passenger jet some thirty-five thousand feet above and who knows how many miles to the north reached his ears as he unscrewed the lid from his flask to pour a cup of coffee. Nibbling on a fruit bar, he took in his surroundings to see what subtle changes had taken place since he was last there. Some branches had fallen into the river, no doubt the victim of high storm winds. The bottlebrush tree had ceased flowering and therefore he noticed a lack of nectar-eating birds and nectar-gathering bees. There was one bird that caught his attention. Sitting on a limb protruding from the stream was an azure kingfisher. A small bird with a breast of rust-coloured feathers, a splash of white and what appeared to be, to Shrimp's mind at least, a coat of brilliant royal blue. With a long stiletto type beak and alert dancing eyes, this pretty little bird was keeping vigil over the river, keeping an eye out for something in the water with which to fill his belly.

Shrimp watched the bird. Studied it without knowing he was doing it. More perfection. Perfect in colour, perfect in its environment, and perfect in its beauty. Subconsciously Shrimp pondered perfect. He pondered the perfects of his past. The perfect fishing trips he'd had on his own. Those with his mates. He pondered the perfect relationships some people had. What was to be his perfect lifelong relationship was stolen from him by illness and a body so wracked by disease she couldn't fight. He had mourned her. He had missed her. But he remembered her perfectly. Would the fish he planned to eat for dinner that night be missed by the fish left in the river? Was it wrong to take some other fish's mother or father, brother or sister from the water, kill it and eat it? From the point of view of the fish, was this a crime? He thought of the perfect crime.

Yes! There was the perfect crime. It was the one case he could never crack. It was a spectre from his early career. As a detective, he had hit his head against a plethora of metaphorical brick walls, but he knocked those walls down brick by brick, head butt by head butt. Often, he had eureka moments while he was doing just what he was doing now. Fishing. It seemed to set his brain into some kind of cruise control, working on a problem, shifting through data while all the time engaged in other activity.

He'd busted drug dealers. He had set honey-traps, using female colleges, to bring down a notorious rapist. Like many in the force, he almost had a respect for some of the small-time career crims and they seemed to have respect for him. Each side of the law knew the rules and, in the main, each side seemed to play fairly.

In all but one case, the perpetrator made a mistake. A slip of the tongue, an inadvertent glance that led to the discovery of evidence, or a raft of blatant lies. As he finished sipping his coffee and reached for his fishing rod, he thought of that perfect crime. The crime he couldn't solve. He knew it was a crime. He knew who committed the crime. He knew! The man who he knew committed this perfection of criminality knew that Shrimp knew, but like Shrimp, knew the copper couldn't prove a thing.

It was the perfect crime.

Then, for no real reason, he thought he just might pick something up from Bishop's clearing sale.

The azure kingfisher unfurled his wings and, in less than a blink, disappeared.

GERALDINE POTTS WAS SMALL, slim and to the men who saw her, perfectly proportioned. At twenty-three, she had avoided many of the temptations of her contemporaries. She didn't indulge in soft social drugs, didn't smoke, and only rarely lifted a glass of alcohol to her lips. She wasn't what some would call a wowser, no, she simply took care of herself and it showed.

Upon completing university, she accepted a position at a country veterinary surgery. The city was home, but her tutors indicated during her final year that experience in the bush would be more satisfying and educational, in more ways than one, than caring for kittens and pampered pups in the suburbs.

As happened in small communities, newcomers were made welcome, and this was the case with Geraldine. Like more than many who had come and gone before her, she appreciated the welcome but often felt on the outer. It was just a feeling. Not that it worried her. She was here to work, not join social circles, no matter how big or small.

The girls at the vet office extended many an invitation for her to join them on Friday nights mixing with others in their age group. Every so often, she accepted. Being new and being attractive, not that she pondered such things, she was a walking pheromone to the young bucks who made their way into town to drink away the week of ploughing, crutching, dipping, sowing, fencing, mustering or any of the plethora of never-ending jobs life on the land dictated, but they were more interested in her than she in them. The girls sipped their drinks, giggled at little immature utterances, and kept an eye out for any attractive boy who may just be on the hunt. They were playing the game, the same game their mothers played, the same game their grandmothers played, the same game played all the way back to Eve. Some of the girls may have been considered easy. Others played hard to get, but they were still out playing the game. Still, others, like Geraldine Potts, were just out.

For Geraldine, it was enough to be out. She avoided hitting town when the annual agricultural show or other crowd attracting events were happening. Too many Mungo-types for her liking. She thought of them as very little advanced from knuckle dragging Cro-Magnons, who, when they managed to get their hands above their waists, only used them for exploring body parts they themselves did not have. Sure, groping may be a part of the game, but Geraldine wasn't playing the game. She was just there. Not even an observer of the game, she was just there.

***

IAN BISHOP WAS A TWIN. Almost identical to his brother, James. In their young years, the only real physical difference was eye colour. Ian had his father's brown eyes, whilst James had inherited his mother's opal blue eyes. To those who knew the Bishop twins these days, they were readily known by their nicknames. Ian was 'Em' or 'Emmie' after the title bestowed upon Bishops of the Church, "Your Eminence" and James reluctantly bore the moniker 'Monk' due to his partial baldness, which started in his early twenties, but put a hat on their heads and if you weren't close enough to see their eyes, they were near enough to being identical.

As the sun was rising, Ian Bishop looked out over his country. Leaning on the verandah rail, he queried himself how many more mornings would he do this. A tidy man, he knew where everything was, on his land, in his sheds, the homestead and his life. That was not quite true. There was one thing in his life that wasn't in place. Surveying Gerry Downs that morning, he pondered, not for the first time, why she left him. Why had she vanished? Where had she gone? Why wait until the wedding day to leave his life? These were questions he'd asked himself over and over. There were also questions the police asked him over and over.

Not for the first time, though, he felt her presence. He had felt it countless times over the past forty-one years. He had felt her close. Close enough to talk to. It was like she was trying to tell him something. Always it was as if she was trying to tell him something.

The purr of the telephone intruded upon his thoughts. It was Monk. The purpose of the call was to see if his brother would divulge his plans. "Come across for a couple of cold and frothies this arvo and we'll yarn about it."

Ian wouldn't, couldn't, make a final decision without consultation with his brother. After all, without James's financial assistance all those years ago, Ian would never have set foot on Gerry Downs. James had generously loaned Ian a quarter of the price of the property, to be paid back in one of two ways. The first was, should Ian pre-decease him, James would receive twenty-five percent of the sale of the place or a quarter of the equity. Secondly, if Ian should ever sell up, James would have himself twenty-five percent of the sale price. That's how it was with the Bishop twins. It was something Ian would never renege on. It was something the brothers never spoke about, each knowing that the hand-shake contract would someday be honoured.

AS HAD BEEN his way throughout life, Shrimp Nolan walked away from every door that closed. He was like that. Once a case was closed, that was it. Nothing more could be done. Even when his beloved Maggie died, and the funeral and wake were over and done with, he closed the door and continued the only way he knew how, forward. Naturally, he drew on the past for the experience it could provide, but he would never reside there. He was also a man who hated loose ends. Despite his haphazard approach to things, he had his way of being, well, compartmentalised, if not tidy.

Tying a different lure, he continued to reflect upon that one perfect crime. He was sure the girl just didn't disappear. He'd heard of women, and men for that matter, getting cold feet and fleeing the altar, but to simply not show up, leave no note and not be seen again reeked of, as is so often reported in the press, suspicious circumstances.

Subconsciously, Shrimp cast and retrieved his lure. Subconsciously, he recalled the facts. It was a long time ago now. What was it? His first case as a young detective constable. If not his first, certainly one in his first year as a D.C.

At the time, he was new at Widenbridge, and the local rag, The Widenbridge Word, carried the story of the social event of the year. Up and coming farmer, son of the local mayor and descendant of an original settler couple from something like

1895 or 96 was set to put a ring on the finger of the local vet's more than capable assistant.

As the event drew closer, the "Word" carried the details in its social/gossip pages. This was to be the biggest event in the district since the Prime Minister and a minor Royal visited about a dozen years previously. The paper carried pictures of the couple at their engagement party, at charity fund-raisers and the annual Combined Service Clubs Ball.

The elegant young vet from the big smoke and the young man on the cusp of a successful farming career, no doubt ready, with his twin brother, to take over the family farm once his father, the Mayor of Widenbridge, and his good lady wife decided it was time to hand things over to the next generation.

Like in any community, there were those who saw things differently. Some, whose circles never intersected with those of the Bishops, claimed he was a sucker for a long leg and a pretty face, while she was just a city tramp out to do some gold digging. Unkind old women and those who knew no better gossiped about the couple and uttered untruths and repeated fallacies and unfounded innuendo. Shrimp smiled to himself as he recalled some of the stories witnesses related during the investigation. He came to hear many such stories over many cases from people who related what he would call, "Somebody saids."

"Somebody said that..."

"Somebody told me in confidence..."

"Only recently I heard somebody say they heard somebody who was talking to..."

He'd heard so much of it and over the years, he'd learned to filter it out. What people often believed to be the truth was in fact misplaced belief and of little use to an investigation, but he had also learnt the knack of filtering out little grains of truth and possible clues.

EM'S BLUE CATTLE BITCH, Jelly, had received a nasty kick to the ribs by a beast in the yards during branding. She was in a bit of a state and would survive, but he thought it'd be best to have the vet check her out. It was decided that they'd finish with the cattle, then they would take the dog into town.

A quick wash under the tank, a cleaner shirt, and it was the forty-minute drive into Widenbridge. James drove. Ian nursed Jelly on his lap and patted her head and told her she'd be sore but alright. The sun was still high in the north-western sky when James swung the ute into Kurrajong Street to find a park right outside the vet's surgery.

The boys went in, Ian carrying the patient. Donna, the receptionist, said, "G'day boys, what brings youse to the living metropolis?"

"Living metropolis!" exclaimed Ian. "I've seen more life at the cemetery."

Donna giggled.

"Jell's copped a flying back-kick from a steer that had some silly idea the branding iron was gunna hurt."

Donna giggled again. "Vet's out at the show ground doing something with pigs that have the runs. I suppose you'd call it pigs' trotters," Donna joked.

Blank expressions from the twins.

"I'll get Geraldine, his new orf-sider."

Geraldine entered through the bat-wing doors from the rear. She saw a distressed Jelly, walked over to the boys and introduced herself. James was smitten from that instant; Ian was more concerned about Jelly. Like a lyrebird trying to impress a prospective mate, James used everything in his hormonal armoury to get Geraldine to notice him.

The young vet smiled. While she examined the bitch, she couldn't help but notice Ian's genuine concern for his working mate. Geraldine had discovered early in her tenure at the Widenbridge Veterinary Hospital that farmers' working dogs were as valuable as anything else they had on their land. James made some remark that almost made the young vet groan audibly. Nearly every boy she had met since her arrival had hit upon her and she was not impressed with this wheat-stork cocky. Turning slowly, she smiled at James and directed his attention to a tortoiseshell moggy dozing in a cage against the wall.

"Nice cat, nice hair cut you've given it," he said disinterestedly.

"It had to be shaved with an Occam's razor. She belongs to the Schrödingers," she said straight-faced. "I have to tell them I have some good news and some bad news about it."

James said he didn't know the Schrödinger's as they must be new to town.

Ian suppressed a laugh, Geraldine noticed, and while she prepared Jelly for an X-ray she noticed other things about the near silent Ian.

SOME MEN PEOPLE just didn't seem to notice; others had a charisma that attracts others to them, whilst there were those who simply have a presence. Sergeant Woo Li Yang of the Singapore Immigration Office was a man who commanded by his presence. His dress, his bearing, his very being gave an atmosphere of command and of needing to be obeyed. Woo Li Yang again examined the photograph as he casually chatted with Passport Control at Changi Airport.

There was a sigh from one particular passenger as Captain Jago Thomas, on behalf of the cockpit crew and the ladies and gentlemen of the cabin crew, thanked all on board the massive Qantas A380 Airbus for flying with them to Singapore. The plane taxied to its terminal and the cabin staff directed passengers from the aircraft while expressing a wish that they'd fly with them again.

A slight nod from a Passport Control Officer alerted Sergeant Woo Li Yang to the middle-aged man with a deep suntan. Woo didn't need the verification; he had his man marked the moment he entered the terminal from the plane.

LIKE EVERYTHING IAN BISHOP DID, he courted with caution and planning. He never went into any situation without intense consideration. Even when playing second row for the Widenbridge rugby team, he gave the appearance to stop in order to weigh up his options in attack or defence. And it seemed to pay off. So it was with Geraldine. He waited for, if not somewhat contrived, the right moment to ask her out the first time. His research turned up a small but interesting fact that the young vet had a creative, artistic bent so, instead of asking her to the pictures, he extended an invitation to attend a semi-classical musical evening, under the full moon, which was an annual charity fund-raiser for children with disabilities, a charity which his father was president and his mother, patron. It was the start of a relationship that was deep but was kept very much to themselves until sometime later, some respectable time later, when Ian calculated and suspected, Geraldine was genuine and wanted his heart and soul, not his name and wallet. He raised the subject of marriage. He didn't propose. He discussed it with her and his parents one Sunday over dinner.

Surprisingly, Geraldine found herself delighted with the situation. She knew by now the kind of man Ian was, so was not taken aback with the practicality of the conversation rather than the flowery, sentimental on the knee marriage proposal of the romance novels and Hollywood movie clap-trap. As the months went by, discussion turned to what the couple would do and where.

"You really should try and branch out on your own place, Em," said his mother, using the familiarity of his nickname.

"I'm aware of that, Mother Dear." He smiled." There've been rumours that old Mr. Beard it thinking of selling, so I drove up to have a chat with him to see what the story was."

"What did Stubble have to say?" his dad asked.

"He's keen to sell, for a price. I know he hasn't really made a go of it, but it has good water, the soil is as fertile as anything about Widenbridge and with a bit of work Gerry and I reckon we could make it work, make it viable."

"You'll need a few quid to get onto it, Son," his father spoke.

"You're telling us nothing, Dad. I've talked to Mr. O'Dell at the Rural Banking Institution and he said if I can knock up a decent deposit, he'll see the bank will come through for us. I wracked my brains to come up with a way to find a ten or fifteen percent deposit, Geraldine offered, of course, but I'm not going to touch any money of hers. Monk and I were mulling it over and he reckons that place of Stubble's is a good bet and he said a little extra mortgage on his place wouldn't be too much of a burden for a brother to carry. He said he'd chip in twenty-five percent to kick us off."

Geraldine's eyes widened. Mrs. Bishop almost dropped

her tea cup. Mayor Bishop let a slight smile escape, but deep inside felt a welling of pride that one of his sons would sacrifice so much for his brother. "That's a shed full of commitment. Can you boys handle it?"

"We believe so, Dad. It will take a lot of work to get the place up to full potential, but it isn't outside the realm of possibility by any means. We have an appointment with Mr. O'Dell at two tomorrow afternoon."

***

THE CLEARING SALE WAS UNDERWAY. The agent was the best in the district, a family friend and a man trusted by the farming community. Everyone knew he'd work hard to get the best price for everything, but then everything deserved the best price. Interested parties from the shire and across the state and beyond were in attendance.

Ian Bishop looked across and saw a face he hoped he'd never have to see again, Dan Nolan. When Geraldine had walked out on him, Nolan had put him, his brother, and his parents under intense scrutiny. Some of the questioning and accusations expounded by the young copper were insulting and without foundation. That was forty-one years ago. That was how the Bishops saw things then and that was how Ian Bishop saw things still. To have a brash full-of-himself policeman investigate as he did was more than they would put up with, and then, at the conclusion of the investigations to have the copper swear he'd prove that his twin brother would be held accountable was more than any reasonable man could accept.

Damn it, the girl had just shot through. Get over it. But Shrimp Nolan wouldn't get over it. He knew there was foul play and he would prove it.

"Leave it alone, Nolan!" exclaimed Ian. "It's been over forty years. Just forget it and get off my place. You're not welcome here and from day one you never have been."

Nolan replied that he was there to see what he could pick up at the sale.

"Nothing in this place is for sale to you."

The sale was an overwhelming success. All that was needed now was the sale of Gerry Downs, and there was a meeting soon with the local stock and station agents, along with a positive prospective buyer. It wouldn't be long and Ian Bishop would settle in Widenbridge town, relax and spend his time on the golf course or bowls green.

Monk, meanwhile, had decided to stay on his own place, but with his twenty-five percent of the sale of Gerry Downs, he expressed his desire to see the world, and, with an upcoming Ashes cricket series to be played in England, he booked himself a six-month holiday in the British Isles and a grand tour of Europe and America.

THERE ALWAYS SEEMED to be something that raised its head at the wrong time. Hours out from the wedding, Monk was lending a hand on Gerry Downs, as Em was rather preoccupied with his impending nuptials. The big dual rear-wheeled tractor needed to have a tyre worked on. An inside tyre at that. It was an annoying job, but one Monk could handle on his own, especially if it was done with the wheel still on the tractor. Bead breaking was something he hated. Handling the wheels on his own would take time, but all he needed to do the job on his own happened to be in the sheds. He swore!

A voice from the yard caught his attention just as the tyre

came from the rim. Pleased with the distraction, Monk wiped his hands down the back of his thighs and looked up to see the woman who would be his sister-in-law this time tomorrow. Following their first meeting, when she so subtlety put him down, Monk thought Geraldine was up-herself. She, at the same time, formed and maintained the opinion that he was somewhat uncouth, although she was astonished by, and grateful for, the generosity shown to his sibling when Ian wanted to buy his own place. Their own place.

"James," she addressed him, "I have to talk to you, for my own peace of mind. I know Em is blessed to have a brother like you. He, we, appreciate what you did to help us get this place, our own home. Em really knows what it means, and I'm sure I will know too what you've done for us. He's a lucky man to have you as a brother. I'm a lucky woman to have him for the rest of my life. As such, I'm fortunate to be entering a family where there is so much love, trust, and respect. From the bottom of my heart, I am honoured to be a member of your extended family and your sister-in-law. I know these are only words, James, but that's all I have with which to say thank you, so, Dear James, thank you."

It seemed that all of Widenbridge and the surrounding towns had turned out for the wedding. The groom and his party arrived in drays drawn by magnificent draft horses. The Bishops had invited both the State and Federal members of parliament along with other dignitaries. The right-hand side of the Church of the Little Flower was near to overflowing. Members of Geraldine's family had travelled from quite far away for her special day. As with most weddings, there was a certain tension permeating the church.

It was such a social occasion that instead of sending his junior journalist and photographer, the editor of the

Widenbridge Word went to cover this wedding himself. He wasn't about to be disappointed.

Ian fidgeted. The priest tried to settle him by saying that it was right for the bride to be late, even this late. Monk, his best man, and the groomsmen joked at Ian's expense.

From the door of the church, a man appeared and motioned to the priest, who went to see what was going on. After a few whispered words, he went back near the altar and took the twins into the Sacristy. Ian physically wilted and wept. The priest addressed the congregation to tell them there'd be no wedding. It appeared that the bride-to-be had a change of mind. A stunned silence lasted until a few seconds later, everybody seemed to start talking at once.

If IAN BISHOP had thought Geraldine's nonappearance at the wedding was as bad as it got, he had yet to encounter a suspicious young detective called Nolan. Not known for tact, Nolan treated the situation of the girl's disappearance as the most awful crime known to mankind. He disbelieved everything they told him. He went over the place with a most quizzical eye. He had the forensic team take fingerprints and tyre prints, hair samples from the bathroom. Geraldine's toothbrush even went to the lab. Nolan sensed murder, and he was out to nail somebody for it.

Day after frustrating day, Nolan searched for evidence. He found none. Mayor and Mrs. Bishop were put under Nolan's microscope. He travelled to the city to interrogate Mr. and Mrs. Potts, the bridesmaids, sisters, friends. Nothing. Not a thing. It all checked out. It was all too neat. Where was she? Why run? Who saw her last? Why were there fresh prints matching her car at the homestead?

Detective Nolan went fishing. He was after a big fish in this case and in order to get his prey, he had to first get his mind in order. He did this on the riverbank. As he prepared his line, he reviewed what he knew. A happy couple on the cusp of a potentially long life together. No harsh words. No car. No girl. No sighting of her, anywhere. No evidence. Only suspicions and suspicions weren't enough.

If Ian Bishop didn't do for her, and Nolan didn't really, in his heart, think he did, then it must be someone close. Who? An old boyfriend? Didn't really make sense. The other Bishop bloke? Something nagged at Nolan. James Bishop had confirmed that his brother's fiancée had been at the property the night before the wedding day and to express her gratitude for what he had done for Ian and herself. Even Monk's good deed stood up, and that annoyed Nolan. There had to be something. What was it?

Teams of police went over and over the place, almost dismantled the homestead, and for what? Nothing! Every avenue was clean. No sign of struggle, no blood, not even a broken twig. Everything at the Bishop place was clean. Neat and clean. Maybe that was it. Too neat, too clean.

With nothing to go on, Nolan could only conclude his report to the coroner that One: The Potts woman had decided against getting married and arranged her own disappearance (Most unlikely. People just didn't evaporate). Two: She met her demise through misadventure, unproven at this stage, as no supporting evidence had come to the attention of the police.

It was like seeing a fish in the river, but getting it to bite was an impossibility. Detective Daniel "Shrimp" Nolan had to let this fish keep swimming, but he made no friends with the Bishops.

Sergeant Woo Li Yang tapped the man on the shoulder. Surprised blue eyes stared at the officer. "Please, come with me, sir." It wasn't a statement; it was a command. Opening a door, Woo indicated the man to sit. Woo left the room, locked the door from outside and went for coffee and a bite to eat.

Time seemed to stand still as an annoyed James Bishop sat in the bare room. He wondered what was going on. The more he wondered, the angrier he became. After ninety minutes, the door opened. The man known as Monk rose.

"Sit!" demanded Sergeant Woo Li Yang.

"What the hell is going on? Why am I here? I've a connection to London to catch." He stood.

"Sit down!" commanded Sergeant Woo. "The answer to your question is two words. Geraldine Potts."

"What? Geraldine Potts, wha? Hey, who… come on, what has Gerry Potts to do with you, or me, for that matter?"

"That is what we intend to find out, Mr. Bishop, and until we do, you are going nowhere. Your Embassy has been advised of your detention and will send an advisor and observer as soon as Australian colleagues of mine arrive. Should you wish to use the bathroom, please say so. It will be arranged, as will some sustenance."

It would be three and a half hours before anything else really happened. Then it was full on. Initially, a representative from the Australian Embassy was ushered in with the observer. James Bishop was informed that his brother, Ian, had passed away a short time ago from a heart attack. Also, extradition papers were at that particular moment being prepared for his return to Australia. He was being held on treaty grounds on the charge of murder. The blood drained from the detainee's face. He began to shake and perspire.

There was a discreet knock at the door. The observer opened it a little and whispered to whoever it was outside. The observer then motioned to Sergeant Woo Li Wang. Woo left the room only to return a very short time later, accompanied by two western men in suits and two uniformed Singapore police officers. One of the men in suits twisted an empty chair the wrong way around and straddled it, resting his forearms across the back of the chair. "I'm Senior Detective Greg Pyke. My condolences on the loss of your brother. My condolences on the loss of Geraldine Potts, whom I'm sure you knew fairly well. Miss Potts' remains were discovered very recently. Do you know where they were discovered, Mr. Bishop? Of course you do. You put them there, didn't you? We haven't found her car, but that's not overly important at this stage. You can fill in that little detail later."

"What happened to Ian?" asked Monk. "He was always so fit and healthy, not a sick day in his life."

The other detective, by the name of Wilburn, said, "You didn't really know your brother then did you, James? He was sick, sick with worry and mystery for forty-one years. Every day for forty-one years, he was sick of not knowing what happened to the woman he loved. He worked his property, named out of love for that woman, every day as if she was there beside him. And you know what, James? She was beside him much of the time, thanks to you."

"You know nothing," said James Bishop, "You're all like that useless clown, Nolan, who fumbled and bumbled his way all over the place looking for a scapegoat. Someone to blame, someone to crucify so he could be number one, the top of the cops. He rushed in accusing every and anyone, put our Mum in hospital, harassed us, the neighbours, and anyone else he happened to take a dislike to, and that was everyone. I've done nothing."

Shrimp Nolan undid his tie as he walked from the Widenbridge Courthouse. He threw his coat on the back seat of his car and drove away to fish and reflect on the events that took over four decades to unfold. All fish can be caught, he reflected. You might not catch them yourself, but given enough time, the fish would fall to the hook and the criminal would succumb to the law.

James Bishop made a few mistakes. He told others of his plans and he flew to places with extradition treaties with Australia. Forty-one years earlier, Geraldine Potts went to make her peace with Monk, for her own peace of mind and for her future husband's sake. She said she only had words with which to thank him. James Bishop thought otherwise and suggested so. Naturally, Geraldine refused such a disgusting offer and, filled with rage, turned to leave. She didn't get far. James reached, grabbed her shoulder, swung her into his vile embrace, and forced himself on her. All her fight had gone by the time he finished. She again turned to flee. This time, Monk stretched out his arm around her neck. He pulled back. There was a crack, and all he had in his hand was a rag doll. A soiled rag doll.

He looked at the body of the woman his brother was due to marry. He picked her up, a small, lifeless lamb. He carried her to the where he was working on the tractor tyre. He was ready to refit the tyre. He could bury her in the crops. He could tie bricks around her and put her in the river. Then he thought, no, she'd be found too easily. He'd think of something. Now grab the little excavator from the other shed, dig a hole next to the pile of cleared trees, bury the car and push the trees on top of the evidence. Leave some scattered about as not to attract attention. Perfect!

It was perfect, thought Shrimp. Perfect until the clearing sale. Just about everything was sold. It would be a few days before the partnership that bought the dual wheel tractor for parts would collect it. By that time, James Bishop would be on the other side of the world enjoying test cricket, his only concern being who would win the toss. Before moving the tractor onto the low-loader for transport, Ian suggested the tyres be inflated. All went well until one of the inside tyres let go with the unmistakable sound of a bursting tube. Ian looked at the tyre. Something thin and white protruded from the rubber.

"Bugger," he thought. "Must be an emu bone picked up in a paddock." An uncommon occurrence but something that did happen. On closer inspection, he noticed the bone was exiting the tyre, not entering it. "Best have a look at this," he said to the crew there to transport the tractor. "Won't take too long."

No one could believe what they saw when the tyre was removed from the rim. Inside was what appeared to be a crushed skeleton. The police were called. As the tyre was examined, one of the police removed a small mangled piece of metal. It was a ring. It was the engagement ring Ian had bought Geraldine all those years ago.

It was then the realisation hit him.

It was then he had the heart attack.

She had never left him. She was taken from him, yet she was always there on the farm with him as she promised she would be. Ian knew that James was changing the tractor tyre the day before the wedding. There could only be one explanation. Only one.

In his hospital bed under the respirators, Ian Bishop asked to see retired detective Daniel Nolan. Shrimp walked into the room with much reservation. Ian extended his hand, expressed heartfelt remorse for the animosity between them, thanked him for the work he'd done all those years ago, then with his last breath said, "Make sure you get the..."

TYING a new lure with a perfection knot, Shrimp Nolan cast into the slow moving, westward flowing Wombadgalong River. He reflected on this perfect day. A slight breeze, not a cloud to be seen, water clear enough to spin in and, for him, not a worry in the world. Shrimp Nolan contentedly sat on the gently sloping river bank. James Bishop sat brooding in a steel and concrete cell.

Sitting on a limb protruding from the river sat an azure kingfisher. "Perfection," thought Shrimp.

THE END

AGAINST THE WIND

t was not just the wind. It was the August wind. That wind that blew from the west. And blew and blew and blew. As far as Retired Detective Daniel Nolan was concerned, it wasn't as bad as the easterly wind. Nolan hated the easterly wind because the easterly wind always seemed to close the fish down, put them off the bite. August had one redeeming feature; the days got longer. The sun rose a little earlier and set a little later. Still, the westerly wind blew and blew and kept on blowing. Nolan, or Shrimp as he was known, loved the thrill of fishing. Always had.

The children and the dogs of Widenbridge were like children and dogs everywhere. Whenever it was windy, they were restless. They played up and were annoying. For some reason, he recalled that titbit of trivia. His neighbour and sometime golf opponent, retired school master Rennie Duff, happened to mention over a beer following a torrid day of trying to break handicap in what seemed like gale force winds that kids, dogs, and horses always played up when it was windy. From then on, whenever there was some trouble with the young people of Widenbridge, Shrimp Nolan always checked the wind and more often than not, it was stronger than usual.

As Shrimp sat on his ice box tying a lure to cast into a quiet, sheltered stretch of the Wombadgalong River, out of the wind, he reflected on how it was restless kids on a windy day who help him solve the robbery of the Widenbridge branch of the Royal Rural Banking Institution. As the retired detective concentrated on tying his lure, his being was filled with bitter-sweet recollections of a time some thirty years, or more, previously.

The crime was one of such precision that the Ds from the big smoke and even a couple of know-all, solve-all detectives from the Federal Police made themselves unwelcome guests amongst the local constabulary and sections of the general community.

Before making his initial cast into the slowly flowing river, Shrimp Nolan allowed himself a rare and brief moment of self-sorrow as he thought of his late wife, Maggie. She was a pretty girl, not in a classical sense, but in a way that made men and women prone to envy, or even jealousy, look twice. She was what was commonly called, in the vernacular, "a bank johnny," a teller. The Royal Rural Banking Institution at Widenbridge was her employer, and it was where the young detective met her on his regular visits to deposit his pay and at the same time organise a bank cheque to post to his widowed mum. Maggie always thought that was a sweet gesture, and she told him so on many occasions. After one such occasion, Shrimp suggested it would be a sweet gesture if she'd accept his invitation to join him for dinner on Saturday night following the rugby game at the Memorial Oval, or the Mem, as the Widenbridge Quolls Rugby Club's home ground was called. The game on Saturday was against arch rivals, the

Daneborough Vikings. He was the referee for the third-grade game.

The retired cop smiled a smile filled with humour and at the same time gave a chuckle of irony as he recalled that it was a wonder pretty Maggie Atherton ever went out with him at all, let alone married him. He wasn't one to dwell on his loss. He accepted that some people, even young people, got sick and didn't recover. He never questioned selfishly, as many do, "Why me?" And neither did she. He did despise the horrid disease that ate away at his wife's physical appearance, but not her inner beauty, or sense of humour, or love for him. He accepted she had died. He accepted that some things he couldn't change, so he concentrated his energies into things he could.

A cockatoo screeched from a hollow high in a gumtree. How this tower of timber, with its massive trunk and branches, leaned over the river without falling was a miracle of nature. Branches, some much thicker than a man, emerged from the main body of this arboreal giant. Some were broken like the twisted hands of a cadaverous witch clutching at empty sky, others, hollowed out, became the nesting home to the native bird life. The squawking cockatoo was answered by its mate, and then a mass of sulphur crested mayhem broke loose.

Shrimp looked up and wondered what the heck had stirred the birds into a frenzy. It may have been a squabble over a nesting site or maybe a prospective mate. Was it mating season for cockies? He didn't know. Were these birds territorial? Again, he didn't know, nor did he know if they were monogamous, as he understood some creatures to be.

"Must be the wind," he thought. "It must send birds nuts too." Then some minute movement caught his eye. What was it? As a detective and an angler, he had learned to be patient, and he had learned to observe. The birds, in their cacophony and aerial antics, were paying particular attention to the trunk of the huge old gumtree. He studied the patterns of the bark, where it had been stripped away in its annual moult, where some of it clung as if afraid of letting go. He studied the subtle shadings and colours, colours that were part of the background of the Australian bush. There, Shrimp saw it. At first, he thought it was a snake, a python, possibly. He kept still, and he kept watch. Any thought of fishing or lures had been relegated to the back of his mind. There!

"Wow!" thought Shrimp, as his eyes focused on what was the biggest goanna he'd ever seen. No wonder the birds were agitated. A lizard that big could easily wipe out the next generation before it hatched. Still, he couldn't change nature.

He cast his lure into the river. His aim, to put it next to the log slightly protruding from the water, was as accurate as a dart hitting a bulls-eye.

SOME YEARS AGO, the main street of Widenbridge was really only busy, traffic wise, for a total of no more than two hours a day. The morning and afternoon peak hours were no more than peak minutes and were at each end of the working day and at lunch time. Parking was no problem. In fact, the council couldn't justify painting parking lines on the road. Widenbridge, while home and work for those who lived there was no Sydney or Melbourne, it wasn't even a Toowoomba, Dubbo, or Bendigo. It was Widenbridge, but it was the commercial centre of the rich agricultural region and the villages nearby.

Jock Rhodes was a schemer, and it was not unknown that his schemes, at times, had landed him in strife. Often over a schooner or five, he'd discuss his latest plan for getting rich. Jock, or Schol to those who knew him, always drank at the Jetty. The Jetty was an old pub with an old name that went back to when Widenbridge was both a Cobb & Co. staging post and a small inland pickup port for barges that ferried wool, wheat, and other produce down the Wombadgalong River to the big river where the paddle steamers collected the cargo for transport to the major markets.

These days there were only three or four decaying pylons of the original jetty poking their heads out from the river surface, like rotted tooth stubs in the lower jaw of a derelict. The Jetty was built towards the end of the 1880s. It was rough then, and in comparison to the R.S.L. or the Brigalow, it was still rough. No amount of metho and elbow-grease could clean the decades of grime adhered to the windows. The hewn timber slat floor was uneven, but some cruelly said it made walking easier when full of the drink. The general perfume of the place permeated the adjacent footpath, and Dorrie, who ran the bar, was as tough as the wrinkled leather skin she was encased in. Still, Schol, his mates and the general no-hopers of the town made the Jetty their own.

Schol was wasting the closing hours of a Tuesday morning yapping with a couple of mates in for the cattle sales. The lads, Plek and Virgil, had unloaded the stock and as they weren't in the market to buy, nor were the cattle theirs to sell, the boss told them to get lost until about three-thirty when they could pick him up at the Brig, with orders not to be late and not to be too pissy.

The conversation had long since gone past girls, dogs, the upcoming race meeting and had turned to the basic financial state of the three drinkers. A dented tin of Dr. Pat with the lid askew and a packet of papers decorated the bar along with their drinks and a bar runner, frayed at the edges, showing faded scenes of Central Australia, its flora and fauna. Lipping a corner of a Tally-Ho and taking a pinch of 'baccy from the tin, Schol rolled himself a racehorse durrie, lit it, coughed and ordered another round. Behind their backs sat a couple of blow-ins killing time rather than out looking for work, if, in fact, it was work they were looking for.

What they were looking for was not what most people would call work.

Sipping on their beer, the locals' conversation about their lack of real money made the strangers half cock their ears. The boys were talking about what jobs made the money. Cattle-cockies topped the list, politicians because they wrote their own perks, the greedy bastards, doctors, overpaid for telling you were sick when you knew that, anyway.

Striking a match and drawing on his smoke, Schol, between drags trying to relight, mentioned working in a bank would be the go. "Twenty here," puff, "fifty there," puff, "do it carefully and no one would be any," puff, "wiser."

Plek reckoned he knew a bloke who'd fill out a withdrawal slip for a hundred, hand it to the sheila behind the counter, chat her up a bit and when she'd ask him how he'd like the cash would casually say, "Oh! Six twenties'd do," and often he'd get away with it. Should the girl be on her guard, he'd then make a joke of it and tease her about being alert and she'd go far in the banking game. They agreed that wouldn't go over with that little honey at the Royal Rural Bank who'd been knocking about with the smartarse copper who spent more time on the river at Mullen's Flat chasing a feed of fish than running down crims, but as far as smartarse coppers go, they agreed, Nolan wasn't a bad bastard.

Nice girl though. Better than old Mrs. Riggs, who'd been there for longer than any of them knew. Cranky old biddy, she was. Then there was the manager bloke, Morrie O'Dell, who also ran the local theatre group and choir. He was not what you'd call a man's man.

"Wouldn't call her a man at all," chipped in Virgil.

The others laughed.

"Ya know, with that kitten running the show, you'd have to fink the Royal Rural would be a push over for any bank-robber werf his salt," said Schol. The other two nodded. The blow-ins looked at each other with raised eyebrows.

A GENTLE MISTY virga started to fall. Soft, soft like the hair of a newborn baby. Dan Nolan cast an eye to the clouds. They were high and drifting, with speed, twisting and tearing themselves on their gust-driven sojourn towards the east. In fact, the sky was as grey as a corrugated tin roof. The birds had quietened their chorus of dispute with the reptile that had either raided enough nests for the time being, or retreated from the onslaught of screeching beaks and aggressive flapping wings. The rain, even though it was light, made it uncomfortable to be on a riverbank that was difficult to traverse at the best of times, let alone with any form of precipitation.

"Best do a goanna," Shrimp mused, and he packed up to head for somewhere more inviting before the heavens decided to open up properly.

With his fishing gear stowed in the boot of his car, Shrimp made his way home. On the way, he drove through the bottle-o of the Brigalow Hotel and purchased a bottle of rum to ward off the cold weather that would surely follow the bout of wet. He stopped by the local bakery for a loaf of unsliced high-top bread and a pie.

At home, he sat on his back verandah and subconsciously

fiddled with some fishing tackle. Having boiled the kettle he made a pot of tea, real tea, using leaf tea, not tea bags, added a tot of the rum to the pot, covered his pie in tomato sauce and added a few drops of Tabasco to give it a kick.

The weather had turned malevolent. He was glad he came home. The wind had changed direction, and the clouds emptied their burden on everything beneath them with a feeling of vindictive menace. The real menace was not in the rain but the wind. It was the wind that set his thoughts on the case from years before, a case that would test, yet solidify, his relationship with Maggie Atherton. A case that had him questioning if he was in the right job, or at least if he was the right man to do the job.

IT WAS A THURSDAY. Most, though not all, of the morning business banking had been done. Personal banking was pretty much taken care of on a Wednesday. The town was quiet. In the bank, Maggie Atherton was at her teller's window. The service bench, constructed of silky oak, carried the aroma of furniture wax. Mrs. Riggs insisted the junior girl, Maggie, polish the barrier, and apply a mixture of methylated spirits and vinegar, with a dash of ammonia, to the glass petitions separating the bank management and staff from their clients each morning prior to the doors opening exactly on the stroke of ten. Deposit slips were in their holders, as were withdrawal forms. Various pamphlets bestowing the wonderments of the Royal Rural Banking Institution and its services were strategically displayed in easy eyeline of those utilising the bank for business.

A door, which was closed more often than it was open, carried the legend "MANAGER - Mr. Maurice O'Dell" in gold-leaf letters. Adjacent to that door, three quarters surrounded by lattice-work varnished and polished to a mirror finish forming an anteroom, a neat desk was situated from which Mrs. Riggs could survey the comings and goings of the customers as well as keeping an overzealous eye on the staff. Mrs. Riggs didn't consider herself as a member of the staff. She was Mr. O'Dell's right hand, his eyes and ears in the service arena of the bank. She was, as she reminded people without prompting, and to use (to her mind) a delightful American expression, the 2.I.C. of the Widenbridge Branch of the Royal Rural Banking Institution. While she was as strict as a school ma'am to the tellers and ledger keepers, she was not above permitting herself liberties she denied her charges. A cup of tea when desired, a packet of biscuits, and a block of sweet milk chocolate resided in her desk's second drawer on the left. Also, it was not unknown that when the local Member of Parliament or the wife of the mayor made a visit to the bank, Mrs. Riggs would be at the enquiries counter to ascertain their business before the swinging doors which formed the bank's entrance closed.

This particular Thursday, Mr. O'Dell was on the golf course. Mrs. Riggs felt it was prudent to represent the bank, unofficially and without invitation, by being seen at the opening of a new branch of a farm supplies store. The opening being conducted by a successful Olympic swimmer, with a number of gold and silver medals to her name, was, apart from possibly being the most recognised and popular person in the country, the corporate face of the company concerned.

The tellers at the Royal Rural Banking Institution were trained to be polite to all patrons, especially polite to new customers, in order to make them feel welcome. More welcome than they would at any another bank in town.

It was a theory that women do not dress to impress men; they dress to impress other women. The swinging doors gave no indication that the person they had just permitted entry to the bank was to cause trouble. She was tallish, a little too full of frame to be called slim, but athletic to look at, exceptionally well dressed, her long fingers sheathed in delicate gloves. When she spoke, it was with a warm and cultured English accent. She was impressive. Naturally, the young girls working at the Rural Banking Institution gave her an admiring once over and the gentlemen working their ledgers had less than professional or gentlemanly thoughts on her figure rather than the figures in their columns.

She smiled at no one in general, looked about, spied the transaction slips, made her way to fill out what was a withdrawal form and, as fate would decree, she made her way to the window with the name 'Margaret Atherton— Teller'. Maggie smiled and, with a pleasant good morning, asked how she could be of assistance. It crossed the teller's mind that the woman seemed to have forgotten her pass-book. In her confident manner, the woman replied that all she required was for the withdrawal to be completed.

Looking at the slip, Maggie saw that there was no name, no specified amount apart from, "all the paper money you have in your till, all the other tills and the safe. Do not concern yourself with coin. Do not activate any alarms. Do not call the manager. I am not alone." At the first sign of protest by Maggie, the woman reached into her basket and showed what could well be the barrel of a pistol.

"Y-y-you c-can't... I-I-I can't do it... I can't authorise such a requisition," she said this loudly enough for her colleagues to hear. The phrase "can't authorise such a requisition" was internal bank code for trouble. One of the men on the ledgers slipped out the rear of the bank. A blow to the back of his head made sure he didn't alert anybody.

"For a smart-looking young girl that was a silly thing to say, ah, Margaret, isn't it? I've been around banks long enough to know the tricks. Now, Margaret, please do what you've been instructed to do and..." The creaking of the swinging doors distracted everyone.

Old Mrs. Woodford, who operated the Coffee Cup Cafe, entered with a thick deposit book and made her way to the counter.

Politely, the woman invited Mrs. Woodford to Maggie's window and took a step to the side. Maggie noticed the woman had put a hand inside the basket. She was meant to notice. The deposit from the old lady took less than three minutes. Mrs. Woodford thanked Maggie and then the tallish stranger and commented favourably on her manners and the charming way she dressed and spoke. The two women exchanged smiles and bade each other a good day.

THE RAIN HAD EASED, but the wind persistently blowing then gusting with a renewed energy to subside and gust again. It was like the powers controlling the weather were using a set of bellows to stir the air.

The wind was not as bad as it was all those years ago when Shrimp stopped to help young Lonnie Quinn. Lonnie's kite was not flying as it should. It would climb just a little, flutter as if it was afraid of heights, then nose dive to the ground. It was a homemade kite. It looked as if it had been around for years. It wasn't flimsy. It was sturdy, of solid construction.

Shrimp hadn't touched a kite since he was a kid, but like

many things in his life, kite flying was integral to his success as an angler.

The next step in the Royal Rural Banking Institution's 'Incident Training' was to keep yourself and others safe. If there was no other reasonable potential outcome, then surrender what had been demanded. This was a step to be avoided, if at all possible.

The woman calmly addressed the staff. She told them that there were others just outside the bank and they were in a position to cause the good employees of the Royal Rural Banking Institution a great deal more inconvenience than they, the staff, could cause them. At that moment the doors violently flew open and the Ledger Clerk, who had slipped out the rear employees' entrance/exit, was delivered back to his workplace sliding across the floor. His bleeding head left a trail of blood.

The girls screamed. Hands flew to mouths. Other clerks made to assist their colleague but were curtly ordered to sit.

"Now Margaret," said the woman, "isn't it about time you acquiesced to what has been requested of you?"

Maggie stood, not in a defiant manner but still in an attitude of one not being subservient.

"Do it girl!" There was a trace of menace, or was it uncertainty in the demand?

Maggie looked at her senior workmates. She was given a nod of confirmation. Only then did she remove the notes from the tills.

"Do not take every note out, my dear. Leave one note of each denomination in its place. We don't want little silent alarms being activated, do we? That could cause much unpleasantness. Now, open this hatch to let me through to help you in the safe." Maggie slid the barrel bolt that held the end of the counter in place. She lifted the counter top and opened the barricade. Stepping into the working area of the bank, the woman purposely studied each member of the staff. One member of the staff purposely studied the woman closely. The women entered the strong room and Maggie collected the paper money as directed.

When the woman was satisfied there was no more to be gained, she, in a manner most uncharacteristic of her demeanour, pierced the atmosphere with a whistle that would have gained the attention of every collie and kelpie within a hundred and fifty yards. As if they were obedient working dogs, two men entered. One from the front, the other from the back. Faces covered with kerchiefs, they said nothing as they produced army surplus knapsacks and filled them with the cash. The men left, not looking once at the staff. The woman added some wads of cash to her basket and made towards the door. Before leaving, she ordered the injured clerk to be taken to his desk and then suggested the counter be closed and bolted behind her.

"Margaret, you have been most cooperative. Thank you." She then removed a note from a wad in her basket and, after folding it carefully with the fingers of her gloved right hand, reached forward and gently placed the note in Maggie's blouse between her breasts. Then, with the index finger of her left hand, tapped the side of her nose. "This will be our little secret. Don't tell that policeman boyfriend of yours." She turned and left.

It began and ended in less than a quarter of an hour.

THE CALL WENT OUT from the Comms Room at Widenbridge Police Station that there had been an incident at the 'Royal Rural'. The two marked cars with lights flashing and sirens crying rushed to the bank. As the unmarked car made the turn into Kurrajong Street, the call came for Detective Nolan to report to Superintendent Patterson without delay.

Putting two and two together and arriving at five, Shrimp feared the worst. An incident at the bank where his Maggie worked and the call back to the station. It could only mean the worst. He told Stan Douglas his Sergeant to drop him at the Royal Rural Banking Institution.

Douglas said "No way, son, you've a date with Curse."

"But, but the bank, Maggie, I mean, I can't just..... Sarg, I have..." he was cut short.

"Sir! You've been ordered back and I'm obligated to get you there. I know you're worried. I'm worried for you, and the lass as well, but you are going to see the boss and that is how it is."

Tony, the duty desk officer, informed Shrimp to go straight to the back office. Knocking on the door, he waited for the invitation to enter. He didn't have to wait long.

Entering his superior's office, he noticed the manager of the Royal Rural Banking Institution and his secretary. What was her name? Higgs? Biggs? Riggs? That was it, Mrs. Myrtle Riggs. Shrimp was not asked to sit. Both Maurice O'Dell and Mrs. Riggs looked ashen. Shrimp's two and two addition was rapidly adding up to six. The Superintendent read the concern on the young detective's features.

"It's alright, Detective, she's safe and unharmed, but she may be in a spot of bother." Shrimp knew better than to ask. It would be revealed to him in the fullness of time. Silence permeated the room.

It was Mrs. Riggs who, somewhat overrun with

enthusiasm or adrenaline, blurted out, "A good sight more than a spot of bother let me tell you. She'll be lucky to step inside a bank, any bank, again; that's if she gets out of prison."

It was too much for Shrimp.

"What is all this about?" he inquired innocently. They all looked at him.

"She's wrapped up in this, and I wouldn't be surprised if you knew something about it," came from Mrs. Riggs.

SHRIMP'S father encouraged his young son on the avenues the boy's life journey took him. Schoolwork, homework, and leisure activities were almost as enthusiastically followed by the elder Nolan as his offspring. An honest man with high scruples, Alan Nolan was the kind of parent who would rather have his children fall from their bikes than have them not ride at all. If there was a boundary of some form, he encouraged his children to not just push it but go beyond it, way beyond it, to create a new boundary. To give young Daniel an idea of how to fight a big fish, Alan suggested they attach a kite to a fishing rod. So with enthusiasm, Dan and his father cut some fine dowel, connected two pieces, crucifix style, surrounded the frame with twine and enveloped the frame in brown paper. To the lower extremity, a length of string extended twice the axis. That formed a flexible spine for a tail of old torn cloth. The flying control line was the fifteen-pound fishing line that was spooled to the bakelite reel seated on the butt end of ten-year-old Dan's four-feet-six-inch fibreglass fishing rod. His proudest possession.

The idea worked. Flying the kite using his fishing rod gave the lad the bonus experience of the having a soaring kite attached to about eighty yards of fishing line whilst giving him the impression, with very little imagination required, that he was fighting a deep-sea whopper controlled by a four-inch side cast reel. Dan Nolan's love of fishing grew stronger from that moment.

***

"NOLAN!" The name was shot at him like a bullet from a rifle. "You are to have nothing to do with this case. You are too close and there are some who have voiced an opinion, one I'm not sure I'm ready to disagree with, that you may be mixed up in this bank debacle." It was Chief Inspector Samuel Philip Ashton who addressed the young detective. Ashton was known by the moniker Bubbles. Not because of his personality, which was anything but effervescent, but simply as a play on his initials. He hated the name, and he hated anyone knowing it. To those who served in the Australian Federal Police under Chief Inspector Samuel Philip Ashton, their boss had no sense of humour whatsoever. This was something the boys stationed at the Widenbridge Police Station were rapidly discovering.

As Shrimp made his way to the door, his boss, Superintendent Patterson, called him aside. "Dan," he addressed the young detective. Shrimp reflected the Curse had never at any stage at his time at Widenbridge called him by his Christian name. "Dan, I'm sorry son. I can't conceive that either you or your sweetheart are involved in this robbery affair. I've been told the city boys will be here tomorrow. It's bad enough having Ashton calling the shots, and it was him who called the H.Q. clowns to join the circus. I'm involved in the investigation, of course, but it appears as no more than the office-boy, I might add, so if there is anything you or Maggie have to say, IF there is anything, say it to me, my boy. Okay? You'll have time to think about it. Although you have my full support, as do all the crew here at Widenbridge, I have to play the game by the rules. I can't stop the two of you seeing each other and I pray you both get through it, but I have to officially inform you that you have been stood down, with pay, until such time this blows over, or you are charged. You can leave your ID card and your firearm with me. Like I said, I'm really sorry son. Watch your step. Watch who you talk to, and I strongly reiterate that if you have any information, you give it to me, not the Feds, not the city cowboys, me! Good luck, Nolan. I think you'll be needing it."

With that, Shrimp thanked his superior officer for having trust in him. He understood procedure. After handing over his ID and pistol, Shrimp Nolan extended his hand, which his team leader shook firmly. Detective Daniel "Shrimp" Nolan exited the Widenbridge Police Station, wondering when, or if, he would return to carry out his sworn duties.

THERE WAS something nagging in the deepest recesses of Maggie's brain. It irritated her in the same manner an itch just below the middle of the shoulder-blades irritates. Was it something the woman said? Was it the way she stood or even moved? What was it?

Over and over again, she replayed the hold up. She had followed protocol. What was it?

Her workmates supported her. The ledger clerk who suffered injury said that if it happened again, he'd not have things play out differently, except for the stitches and the mighty headache. It was he who raised the question of Mrs.

Riggs and what support she had given the young teller. Maggie knew the answer to that. Absolutely none! What was it with the stuck-up old biddy? And what was it, that like that itch, she couldn't reach?

Oh! What was it?

AT ABOUT HALF-PAST two the following afternoon, Shrimp, head bowed, wandered along Kurrajong Street until he reached the intersection with Loading Street, where he had his flat. Instead of turning north to go home, Shrimp made his way south towards the river. A minute or two later, he was in the shadow of the Jetty Hotel. A blue heeler and his crossbred mate both lifted their heads and regarded the intrusion into their slumber through dust-filled eyes that hardly saw what they were looking at. A yap from the blue dog, but not even a tail wag from the dun-coloured mongrel with flies hovering like miniature vultures around the corners of his saliva-dripping mouth.

Looking through the half-raised sash window, Shrimp spied a familiar figure drinking alone. No one bothered to look up as he entered the Jetty. He hooked a foot around a stool and drew the seat to himself. He climbed on, put a mid-denomination note and some coin on the bar and ordered two schooners in reply to Dorrie's double-edged enquiry, "Strewth, Mr. Nolan, what brings you inta here and what's ya havin' a fill of?"

"This place is a bit too classy fer your type, ain't it Nolan? Ain't ya got no fish that need catchin'?"

"Not today, Schol, not today." He passed the second glass of beer to the man on his left.

With a mock yahoo Schol Rhodes announced to nobody

and anybody that he'd just won the lottery and the copper had bought him the ticket. "Yer in a bit of a generous mood," the layabout said.

"No, not really," said the policeman. "Just need to clear my head a bit."

"Drink too much of this stuff an' yer'll only fog yerself up in the 'ed," was Schol's reply. "Bit ov a nasty caper wiv that sheila ov yours an' the Rural. Few stories floatin' about, an' you feature in a couple ov 'em. Not that I'd say fings like that."

"Like what exactly, Schol?"

"Like that bit o'tail you knock about wiv bein' in on the 'do over' an ow you coulda been in on it. Not that I'd beleef it, Nolan, I reckon yer both too straight for that. Still, like me old mum use ta say, 'Ya never can tell, Jock, me boy, ya never can tell.'"

Shrimp deliberately drained his glass slowly, keeping his eyes focused over the glass tube and on the man next to him. Rhodes looked around the public bar of the Jetty Hotel, then looked at the empty glass on the bar. Nobody was paying any attention to the two perched on ancient stools because, apart from Dorrie behind the bar, there was no one else to notice anything.

"Stuff you, Nolan, waddaya fink people'd fink of me shoutin' a bleedin' walloper a drink? Hey! Dorrie, it's startin' to break inta drought down here."

Shrimp couldn't help but smile at the turn of phrase.

THE DRIVE from Widenbridge to Daneborough wasn't a long one, but it was very pretty: about forty minutes through sparse native forest flanked by the generally lazy flowing

Wombadgalong River, along which the Sentimental Highway roughly ran in parallel.

"We studied the works of C.J. Dennis in early high school," Maggie said, "but I never realised that his most popular work was honoured by this roadway."

Shrimp smiled at her. "I don't know too much about him myself. I've probably heard my old man rattle off one or two of his verses. He was like that with my Dad. At the drop of a hat, he'd start sprouting poetry. We made sure we never dropped too many hats."

Maggie opened up with a laugh. "You're an idiot," she said. "But at least you're my idiot."

Small talk filled the journey to Daneborough. Little cries of delight from Maggie each time she spied the flying rainbows of the parakeets. Shrimp informed her the pretty ones were the males. The females were often dull, in many instances brown, to camouflage nests and young. At one stage, a flock of about a dozen galahs appeared out of nowhere and flew dangerously and acrobatically around the car. They both ducked out of reflex.

"Careful Dan," Maggie warned.

"If ever there was a creature more aptly named, I'm yet to come across it." Shrimp laughed.

Maggie was a little surprised when Shrimp parked outside a store that specialised in baby clothing and other infant paraphernalia. She was even more surprised when the woman behind the counter addressed him as Detective Nolan and handed him a package, which Shrimp paid for.

"Kiddies' slippers," was all he said to Maggie, who raised her eyebrows in as if in question. He then let her take him shopping, after which she allowed him to take her to lunch.

THE FEDERAL POLICE seemed more concerned about the movement of the stolen money. Their team interviewed most of the staff of the Royal Rural Banking Institution. They compiled information on the bank's small customers and major business clients. They took notes on when cash moved into and out of the bank via armed security. They made a detailed inventory of serial numbers, denominations and amounts of each denomination stolen. Ledgers were confiscated, time sheets dating back twelve months were taken for forensic examination, and questions asked as seemingly banal as to where staff members took their lunch and with whom they spent their meal times.

It was left to the city detectives to look into the criminal aspect of the case. Their attitude was most unwelcome, not just by the Widenbridge Police, but by the community in general. The city team displayed, for any who cared to see or listen, a demeanour of, "We know what we're doing, keep out of our way and let us solve this before lunch on Friday so we can get home for the weekend."

Superintendent Patterson explained to the senior detective investigating the actual robbery that he'd already had spoken to Detective Nolan. He was then told, in an unforgiving manner, that asking your mate a few routine questions over a drink in the beer garden of the local pub didn't constitute, in their opinion, a right and proper interrogation. This is a real crime, he was told, not something as simple as finding a few cows missing from Farmer Freddy's back paddock. That did nothing to endear themselves to the local law enforcers.

"Just tell us the truth, Nolan. You should know how this works. Tell the truth and things will go easier for you. That girlfriend of yours is being spoken to and broken by our team as we speak. So, let's just get to the point. We both know that you and, what's her name, Margaret, were in on this bank job.

How the hell did you think you'd get away with it? I cracked bank jobs before you even knew what a bank job was, sonny-boy. I can spot a put up when it's staring me in the face and I do believe I'm being stared at by one now."

Shrimp rose from his chair, hands gripping the table edge in the manner an eagle's talons grip an unfortunate leveret. His eyes narrowed to slits as his brow furrowed in an amalgam of frustration and anger. Before any words could come from his mouth, he was ordered to sit down in the attitude a drover would yell at a recalcitrant blue cattle pup.

"Listen to me, Nolan, with me you're not a colleague, you're not a big frog in your sleepy valley fishpond, you're a suspected criminal. In my eyes, you're a guilty criminal at that. All I have is suspicion and you are very lucky that's not enough to hold you on, let alone charge you. You are the lowest of the low, Nolan, a bent cop. You may think you're clever, but you ain't clever enough for me, pal. If you think I'm going to treat you rough, just wait until you get inside. Those boys behind bars will have a field day with you when they discover you're a cop and I wish I could sell tickets to watch the show."

There came a knock on the interview room door. The city detective opened the door and spoke to someone unseen who spoke just loudly enough for Shrimp to hear the words, "The woman has all but confessed."

A smile formed on Shrimp's lips. He knew the game. He himself had used the ploy, so he knew he had to outbluff those up-themselves Ds from the big smoke who had shown no respect for their country colleagues or for the way an investigation should be conducted.

As he wasn't involved, he knew Maggie couldn't and wouldn't give those interviewing her any satisfaction as far as involving him in the crime. Naturally, they were accused of colluding and concocting their stories. In the time since the holdup, Maggie had gone over and over the circumstances of the incident with Shrimp. He questioned her as a friend, as a detective, unofficially, and as one would question one who was guilty of being involved. To that line of investigation, she took great exception.

There was no joy in Shrimp's method. He grilled her without compassion. She was so shocked at some of his tactics that she questioned how a man who claimed he loved her could be so callous. She didn't know he was questioning himself about the way he, as an upholder of the law, was coldly applying that law to get some kind of result. He hated himself. Not for the interrogation, but for her tears, her trembling, her sudden emotional turn around towards, or rather away from, him. There was nothing in her answers to his questions to indicate any criminal involvement. That was the conclusion rapidly being reached by those conducting her interrogation. They never told her that and they weren't going to tell Daniel Nolan. They had them guilty, and they were doing their best to nail them.

They were the only suspects, uncertain suspects at that, so both were released under instruction to stay close in case there happened to be more questioning. And there would be more questioning.

Over a beer and a shandy, Shrimp and Maggie discussed events and eventualities of those events. Maggie's nagging itch of a thought seemed to be getting closer to the surface. Shrimp told Maggie of the two strangers who were drinking in the public bar of the Jetty. Shrimp said that Jock Rhodes couldn't really describe them but he thought it more than a coincidence that the Royal Rural was done over two days after he and his mates were chatting about how to pilfer a few dollars from a bank if you happened to work in one.

Maggie's interview with the city cops was rough, just as rough as what Shrimp's had been. She was accused of being in on the robbery. In fact, being a mastermind of the robbery.

The detective interviewing her, with a junior police woman in attendance, worked an angle that the woman involved as the perpetrator of the hold-up seemed to know her way around the bank, knew that there was a rear staff entrance, knew the holdup code and, no doubt, knew Miss Maggie Atherton. She knew, too, about the silent alarms and knew that she, Maggie, had a cop for a sweetheart. What the interviewing detective didn't know, and he was sure Maggie did, was how the woman knew so much. The intense questioning focused on Maggie's alleged association with the woman.

Naturally, others were spoken to by the police. Of course the manager, Mr. O'Dell, was as helpful as he could be, and Mrs. Riggs, while being sugar sweet to the city detectives who interviewed her, was nothing less than scornful of the young teller Margaret Atherton. The phrase, "Surely that young Miss knows something, she must!" made things worse for Maggie, and reinforced the detectives' belief that Maggie was in on the job when they spoke to Mrs. Woodford. Without knowing it, the coffee shop owner made things far from comfortable for the young bank teller by claiming that Maggie and the woman seemed to have some kind of friendly rapport. Maggie kept denying any knowledge of the robber, but did say there was something vaguely familiar with her.

Something, but what? That "something" was the straw the interrogating detective clung to.

THE STORM CONTINUED to dump rain on Widenbridge. The clouds threw lightning to the ground as whalers of old would hurl harpoons. With each bolt there came the inevitable concert of thunder. Still, the wind unsettled the trees, the power-lines and the few loose papers littering the streets.

Shrimp didn't mind the storm. It was background as he worked on his fishing equipment with the same enthusiasm he had as a ten-year-old. Flakes of pie pastry and sauce decorated the old rugby jersey he was wearing. Steam from his rum laced pannikin of tea rose slowly, like smoke from an awakening volcano, to be sent to oblivion by the wind. Grey stubble filled the creases of his face where yesterday's razor failed to shave. Parallel furrows came and went between his eyebrows as his eyes worked to see some detail of his project.

"HALF THE PROBLEM," Shrimp smiled up at Lonnie, "is that it's too windy and the wind direction is inconsistent."

"So it isn't she's too heavy, or the tail is short or somethin' then, Mr. Nolan?"

"It is a bit solid, but it should fly under ideal circumstances."

Just then, a couple of Lonnie's mates rode up and with the cheeky attitude of small-town kids, with just the right touch of respect, stirred Lonnie about crawling to the cops.

The young Wilson boy, too skinny to cast a shadow, hair whiter than an angel's robe and carrying the nickname Darkie, jibed Shrimp with the comment, "Couldn't lend me twenty, could ya, Mr. Nolan?"

His mates knew what he was digging at and so did Shrimp.

"Sorry, Dark, but poor old country coppers don't make that sort of money. At least not enough to throw away on a reprobate like you."

His mates laughed at the policeman's retort.

"Yeh! But what about poor old country bank robbers? I bet they make that sorta money."

"Maybe I need a career change then, Darkie. Waddaya reckon?"

"Me 'n the boys here reckon it's a bit rough on you an' Miss Atherton, we know ya would'na dunnit. All Widenbridge knows ya gun-barrel."

"Thanks boys, appreciate that. If only you could convince the visiting fuzz. Where are you lot off to on a day like today?"

It was Lonnie who answered. "Three o'clock Saturdee arvo, Master Garry 'Darkie' Wilson esquire and his faithful entourage would no doubt be making tracks to the town hall stage for rehearsals of an upcoming Widenbridge Theatre Group production of which the aforementioned shy, but talented, Master Wilson is scheduled to lend his fine tenor register and thespian skills to said production starring and directed by Widenbridge's leading talent, none other than Mr. Maurice O'Dell."

They all laughed.

"Fair dinkum Dark, you treading the boards?"

"Like none other, Mr. Nolan, like none other. In fact, why don' cha come and see it? Me mum reckons you could do with a bit of distraction. We open in a fortnight and ya can get tickets at the chemist or the rural supply shop."

"I just might do that, Darkie, my boy, I just might do that," Shrimp thought to himself as the boys mounted their bikes and rode away. He and Lonnie then turned their attention back to the kite.

IT WAS the next best thing to being a dead end without really being one. There were no new clues, no change of stories, and only rumour and speculation, which are not ideal ingredients in the recipe of investigation. The majority of the Federal Police had left Widenbridge, the city detectives had exhausted all avenues to explore and to the dismay of the police, and their main suspects, old ground was being rehashed to no avail. The only glimmer of hope in the investigation was in the initial days following the hold up, when some of the stolen notes made their way into general circulation. This was all but dismissed by the investigators as normal spending by the perpetrators.

Dan Nolan was still on leave with pay. Maggie was issued full suspension from the Royal Rural Banking Institution, which to her mind, equated to a permanent severance. Mr. O'Dell seemed content to have the police try their best to track the woman and her henchmen, while Mrs. Riggs was quick to condemn the young teller and her beau to anyone who'd give an ear to her bitter speculation.

THE WIDENBRIDGE THEATRE Group was a vibrant and active performance group offering the community drama, comedy, musicals, farce, and recitals. Maurice O'Dell was passionate, if not obsessive, about the theatre group. For some years he had been the guiding hand and main promoter of local talent. There was no doubt about his skills, on stage and off, acting, singing, directing, writing, stage managing, lighting, sound, wardrobe, and makeup. Maurice O'Dell could do it all and do it very well.

Those who attended any of the six performances of Double Dutch, a play with a twist or two or three, were engrossed in the multi-layered plot, the confusion cleverly portrayed through the storyline and the quality of the songs and the singers.

Maggie claimed that there were really only two nights to see a local play production. They were the opening night and the last night. Most other stagings were entertaining, in her view, with the exception of the second night which, following the euphoria of the opening for the cast and crew, often fell flat. Second night syndrome, she called it. With that as her mindset, it was decided that she and Shrimp would attend the final performance.

The play was performed faultlessly. As it is with local theatre, after the final bows, the actors and backstage people mingled with the audience, shared observations of the production and talked about logistics of staging such a show. There were the usual questions from the public like, 'How do remember all your lines? Do you forget your words? What happens when you do? Who works out who stands where?' et al.

As the leading actor and the director was the one and the same Maurice O'Dell, Maggie thought it prudent that she and Dan not mingle after the final curtain.

<hr>

HIS PIE CONSUMED and the last of the tea drained from the pot, Shrimp cleared the lunch things, such as there were, from the table and continued working on his fishing equipment. Reels needed respooling with new braid line, leader was required and new lures unpackaged and stored in his tackle box.

Still the wind kept blowing and still Shrimp reflected on that case from so long ago and within that reflection were memories that made him smile unconsciously.

WALKING hand in hand towards the late closing cafe on Kurrajong Street, they discussed the play, singing snippets of songs laughing and quoting lines from the play. Entering the cafe they made their way towards a booth by the window and waited to be served. It was a little tradition with them that Shrimp would order for the both of them. This evening, and being in a playful mood, Shrimp suggested Maggie do the ordering.

"No, Dan, that's your job."

Quoting a line from the play, he came back with, "Isn't it about time you acquiesced to what has been requested of you?"

Maggie froze. "What did you say?"

He repeated the line.

She paled, shook her head, looked at him and smiled. "You genius Detective Daniel Nolan, you absolute little trimmer. That's it! That's what has been nagging me these past few months. That's what I've been trying to find, that missing element from the hold-up."

"What is it, Maggs?"

MILT DE GREY, the leading journalist working on the Widenbridge Word, greeted Dan and Maggie at reception and invited them down to his office. He moved a pile of a dozen or so editions of the Word from the spare chair and acquired another from the next office. "And what is it that I should be summoned by Bonnie and Clyde?"

Both Shrimp and Maggie exaggerated a sigh but smiled all the same.

Dan answered. "Milt, at this stage I want your word this will stay in this office for the time being. It's early days yet."

"This has to do with what happen at the Royal Rural?" asked de Grey.

Shrimp nodded.

"Well, it kind of goes against my sticky beak nature, but if, if, there's a bigger story at the end of it, and you promise it will be my story, no leaks to the city papers, the local radio or the tele, than any ears these walls have are deaf."

"Good enough for me," said Shrimp.

Maggie smiled and nodded.

"Here!" de Grey cried. "I knew there would have been some photos."

"This is certainly the day that the Olympics girl came to town to open that new rural store. See, there? That's the Riggs woman."

All three studied the photos.

"These weren't in the paper, Milt?" asked Maggie.

"No, love."

"Any idea what time these were taken, mate?"

"No. Why?"

"Well, it seems to me that in quite a few of these snaps she's spending a lot of time looking at her watch."

THE WIDENBRIDGE POLICE Station snapped to attention when Chief Inspector Samuel Philip Ashton entered the building. No pleasantries were exchanged as he snapped to the desk attendant to get Nolan in here now, as well as the girl. Superintendent Patterson stormed out of his office wanting to know what the ruckus was all about when he spied Ashton. Leading his Federal colleague into his office he was then briefed and updated on the latest developments in the robbery. It was a polite call that Maurice O'Dell received inviting him to Widenbridge Police Station to discuss one or two details of the robbery some months earlier. Without O'Dell's knowledge Mrs. Riggs was also invited to pay a visit to have an informal chat with Superintendent Patterson. Both arrived at the station within ten minutes of each other and were taken to separate offices. Each not knowing the other was there.

ONCE AGAIN SHRIMP and Maggie were driving up to Daneborough. "Daaaaan?" Maggie asked with a childish sing-song inflection.

"Yeess, my love?" he replied mockingly.

"You don't have any nieces or nephews, do you?"

He said he didn't.

"Who then do you know with a baby?" she inquired.

Shrimp replied he knew nobody with a baby. He smiled and said, "What's with the interrogation about babies?"

"It's just that last time we came up here you collected a pair of kiddies' slippers and I was wondering about that?" She almost jumped off the seat as Shrimp exploded in laughter.

"I didn't want baby slippers; I just wanted the little bells they put on the top of the slippers. I attach them to the tip of my fishing rod, as an alarm, when I fish at night, so I know when I get a bite. I get the bells and the fish, the Salvos get the slippers which I hope go to some littly whose mum can't afford 'em."

A burst of siren interrupted their conversation. Pulling over they were joined by a squad car driven by a young constable. "What's up Rodge? Was I speeding?"

"No, sir, Mr. Nolan, there's a bit of a general call out for you and ah, Miss, ah Miss, your friend, to report to the station pretty quick. Don't know what about but evidently that big wig fed is calling for you."

"Thanks, Rodger, I'll swing about and head in. Maggie, this could be it!"

SUPERINTENDENT PATTERSON MADE sure Maurice O'Dell was comfortable, a cup of tea, a biscuit and an atmosphere of friendly relaxation. Small talk about the success of the play was the topic. The door opened, Patterson rose and introduced Chief Inspector Ashton, who apologised to Maurice O'Dell for interrupting. O'Dell smiled, shook hands with Ashton and mentioned that they had met not long after the incident at the Rural Banking Institution a few months back.

Patterson smiled and said to the Chief Inspector, "We were just yarning about the local theatre group and the play they have recently staged. Maurice here, directed and played the lead character. Very good, he was, Chief Inspector."

"I dabbled in a bit of acting myself in my university days," said Ashton, "but I could never get into being someone else. I always thought it was me being me saying something someone else might say. How do you do it, Mr. O'Dell? How do you somehow change from being you into being somebody else?"

"Ah! Chief Inspector, I believe that in order to convince the audience you first must convince yourself. If you believe you are the character, then others will believe. One person could be many people."

"So, what you are saying is, let's see, if you, Maurice O'Dell wanted to be a Frenchman you could?"

"Oui."

"Or an Indian?"

"Most certainly, Sahib."

"What about a child?"

"Not impossible, but physically demanding. Makeup would be heavily utilised."

"Surely you couldn't pass yourself off as a woman?"

"If the role demands it of course, easily. Ah, um, ah that is more easily said than done even for the most experienced of actors, actors with a wider talent than I'd, um, ever dare dream to possess." Maurice O'Dell suddenly felt he'd been led into a trap and hoped against hope that he managed to talk his way out of it.

"Fascinating, makes sense. I wish that had been taught to me back then, well, very good to meet you again, Mr. O'Dell. Sorry to interrupt, Superintendent." And with that Chief Inspector Ashton left the room. Superintendent Patterson took a mental note of the barely noticeable sigh of relief that escaped from the manager of the Royal Rural Banking Institution.

IT TOOK a little digging but Milt de Grey found what he was looking for, or rather didn't find what he was looking for. The Widenbridge Word was a locally owned and operated newspaper of some quality and pride. It covered events, not just in the town, but in the entire surrounding district. Major news, local interest stories, without bordering on gossip, social, and sporting matters. It was the latter de Grey was researching.

Going back over recent archives, he searched and searched the golf results from the time of the bank job. There was golf played throughout the district that day. Maurice O'Dell, a more than handy golfer, with a handicap of seven, who, week after week, featured in the top results, never rated a mention on the day in question. De Grey asked about, dug around and discovered that O'Dell had indeed turned up prepared to play, had even paid his green fees before apologising to his team mate and opponents that something had upset his digestive system and even the first tee, let alone the middle of the back nine, was too far away from where he was likely to be spending much of his day, so he took his leave.

BOTH PATTERSON and Ashton were seated in Patterson's office when Shrimp knocked on the door. He was told to enter and both he and Maggie went in. "You were ordered to stay off this case Nolan," was fired at him as he walked into the office.

"Yes, sir! That's correct."

"Then how come you appear to have turned up evidence when the city boys and the Federal Police failed?"

Shrimp explained about attending the play, the throwaway line in the cafe, and the connection made by Maggie.

Superintendent Patterson informed the chief inspector that he personally requested Nolan to keep him updated on anything related to the case that he, Nolan, in his day-to-day activities may have uncovered. While technically on leave, as a policeman he worked the code that a copper is always on duty and he did all he could to steer away from the investigation worked out of the station at Widenbridge. He did follow one or two avenues to try and deflect the incriminating evidence away from Maggie. He held nothing back. There was no point as his superiors knew of every move he'd made from the conversation with Jock Rhodes to putting Milt de Grey on a very thin trail. Shrimp explained he didn't have all the answers, in fact he really had no answers, but he had strong suspicions and was happy to share them with Patterson, Ashton, or whoever else cared to lend ear.

"Well, Nolan, Miss Atherton, please sit down and we will give you some answers. As it turns out, Miss Atherton, your observations and attention to detail, while pointing to yourself as a strong suspect, showed the cleverness of the crime. Nolan the little information you gleaned from Mr. Rhodes was enough for forensics to lift prints from the table where the two strangers were seated. Smart crew at forensics. While the glasses the two drank from were washed and the table top wiped down, the fingerprints team lifted some very clean prints from under the table rim. Seems these two are nephews of Mrs. Riggs. As it turns out she happens to be a rather avaricious piece of work and I don't know if you know, or suspected, but the Riggs woman is, or now maybe was, romantically involved with Miss Atherton's bank manager, Mr. O'Dell."

Shrimp and Maggie looked at each other and both raised their eyebrows.

"Well, well, well," said Maggie.

"Well, well, well, indeed Miss Atherton, and it appears that their pillow talk was a little more than sweet nothings. The two nephews both have form interstate, both were up to adventure, and were no problem to recruit. Now, according to O'Dell's version of events, the Riggs woman put it to him to see how far he could carry out his acting skills. It was a challenge O'Dell rose to.

"They had even worked out a contingency of using the robbery as an unscheduled security exercise should things not go to plan. As you know they didn't. The grievous bodily harm charge stemming from the bashing of the ledger clerk will not go down well with the judge. Now! It was Miss Atherton's observations, as I said, and her recalling that particular line from the play that really brought this home to roost."

"I beg your pardon, Superintendent, but it was Dan, ah Detective Nolan, who quoted that line."

"That may be so, but it was you who recalled what the woman—well man dressed and acting as a woman—said during the robbery.

"Anyway, O'Dell and Riggs were the masterminds, and they almost got away with it. I've spoken to the State Manager of the Royal Rural Banking Institution, who tells me you followed and adhered to all protocols laid down by your training, probably a little more rigidly than Detective Nolan followed directives from this office, but without which we wouldn't be where we are now. Don't smile Nolan, there will be some repercussions concerning your actions. Where were we? Oh yes, it was a clever plan, both had a fairly solid alibi, but not solid enough to withstand the scrutiny of Mr. de Grey. It goes to show that our work would be more difficult if not for conscientious members of the community."

Putting his fishing reels into their padded pouches and cleaning up the detritus of his afternoon work, retired detective, Daniel "Shrimp" Nolan watched as the wind forced the treetops to dance against their will. He thought it strange that he would recall that case from so long ago.

He thought of the tough times he and Maggie went through. He thought of the repercussions his boss spoke about and uttered a quick laugh, it was the first time he'd ever heard of repercussions being two weeks of paid leave.

Other thoughts leapfrogged over each other. He recalled the windy day Lonnie Quinn had trouble flying his kite and how he, Detective Nolan, suspended, stopped to lend a hand. He remembered the other boys who stopped by to stir Lonnie about being pally with a cop. The throw away suggestion from Garry Wilson that he attend the play the Widenbridge Theatre group was staging. The line in that play that was the loose piece of wool which, when tugged, unravelled the Royal Rural Banking Institution robbery.

Again, he looked at the windblown trees and he thought, with a smile, how Margaret Atherton had blown into his life and how even now, many years after her death, she filled his heart and his thoughts. With his hands firmly gripping the rail running the length of his verandah he gave thanks for the wind that blew such pleasant memories into his life.

THE END

THE DEALER'S HAND

Not often enough, Shrimp Nolan enjoyed rolling out his swag by a river. He relished feeling the freedom of nature as he cooked the fish he'd caught that day in an old pan over a campfire of dry, broken branches he'd collected along the riverbank. The smoke permeated his clothes and his hair—what there was of it.

Like everybody, Shrimp had trivial regrets in his life. One such regret was so trivial that whenever he reflected upon it, he would utter an almost school-girlish giggle of self-embarrassment. That regret was that he couldn't sing. He'd even laughed out aloud when he recalled the words of his late wife, Maggie, that he couldn't carry a tune if it was in a suitcase. Still, it didn't stop him humming a tune or belting out a random chorus of some song that mistakenly made its way into his head and out of his larynx.

He found one of life's simplest pleasures, one that cost nothing and hurt no one, was to lie on his swag under a moonless night sky. He'd lose himself and become absorbed in the starry firmament. To catch a shooting star as it ignited in the upper atmosphere was a wonderment without end. A major part of the wonderment was not hearing that heavenly body as it scarred, if only for a moment, the night sky in perfect silence. During such a time he felt like he was the only person alive. He was alive. On occasions he'd fallen asleep under the heavens to be woken by a gentle damp of a settling dew.

Listening to the bush at night, he thought, must be akin to listening to the voice of God. Possums calling to each other, koalas with their angry mating grunts, the dull thud made by wallabies and kangaroos as they navigated the scrub, the insects, the night birds and even the song of the river as it journeyed its way to the west, added to the voice of the night. Then there was another sound. A sound not heard too close to town, but as one went out into the wilderness, there was the chance the warrigal's howl would chill the bones. In the dark hours before the sun illuminated the eastern horizon, was there a more mournful cry?

Funereal is the howl of the dingo.
Wild dog of bush and desert sand hill.
Heart stopping, that cry of that dingo,
On nightly prowl, out prowling to kill.

It was a verse his father had recited when Shrimp was young and the pair were camping outback on a western station owned by a friend of the senior Nolan. Shrimp had no idea who penned the verse or if it just rolled off his father's tongue. Shrimp had known some dingoes during his career as a copper. Petty thieves, pimps, conmen and women, but none as low as drug dealers. One drug dealer in particular was the lowest of the low, so low that the dingoes on four legs would never be as snivelling as Sean Crosby.

Levels of corruption permeated all societies. Some was highly masterminded, some simply evil personified. Sean Crosby could be classed as such. He was devious, intelligent, without being wise, and had nobody's welfare in mind except his own. Worse of all was the fact that he possessed a magnetic personality, a charisma. He could hold his own in conversation with political leaders, churchmen, business executives, professionals, tradesmen, and the common worker. With a different outlook on life, Crosby would have been more than a valuable asset to any community.

Like all towns, Widenbridge had its fair share of societal scum and lowlifes. Petty crims, teenagers venting frustrations, and true bad eggs with charges of rape, grievous bodily harm, arson, and more against them. These were also often attracted to the charm of Sean Crosby. It was with the likes of the Widenbridge dregs that he preferred to spend his time.

Crime in Widenbridge was kept fairly well in check by the local constabulary. The constabulary was always being checked by Sean Crosby.

It was not without reason that Crosby was not behind bars. His cunning approach to his trade was unparalleled by those who considered themselves his peers. Every nefarious activity he planned had built-in trapdoors and escape routes, physical and metaphorical, designed to keep him out of court and thus, out of gaol. That was not to say he wasn't known to those sworn to upkeep the law, just the opposite. He was very well known and whether he suspected or not, there was always a close eye peering at Sean Crosby. Sometimes that eye was closer than even he could have imagined.

Psychologists may have blamed an unstable family background, an incident that triggered a path away from a social norm, or a traumatic event in early childhood for the way Sean Crosby happened to be. Truth was, he was just a bad man. His father was a successful businessman running a rural supply outlet. Mrs. Crosby kept home, gave time and energy to many of the local charities, attended church and even held Scripture study in her home. Crosby's brother was studying architecture at university and his sister had married into one of the district's leading farming families. No, there was nothing but love and nurturing in Sean Crosby's history.

From his early days at school, he picked his targets with accuracy. The gullible were easily coerced into doing Sean's dirty work. All the time he kept himself distanced from the schoolyard crime he had initiated. It seemed that nothing could stain his character.

One thing the young bounder could not have possibly banked on was the fact that young victims have memories that stay with them into adulthood. While Sean Crosby, the schoolboy, was making mischief, he was also making enemies.

AFTER SCRAPING the inedible remains of his dinner into the fire, Shrimp filled two billies and put them to boil. One would be used for a brew of tea and the other for his camp domestic duties of washing up and a quick clean up.

With the 'housework' seen to, he made sure the fire couldn't escape and settled into the evening. Should he be awake prior to sunrise he half planned to wander to the river's edge and spend the final period of pre-dawn darkness fishing with a surface lure. The object of the surface lure was to make as much noise and disturbance to attract a fish, preferably a big fish. Some surface lures resembled little fish, others, snakes, frogs, and even rodents swimming from one bank to the other. Shrimp was not alone in thinking that catching a fish on a surface lure in the dark could almost be as exciting as fishing gets. The choice of lure, the cast, the retrieve that leaves a wake and then, if all went to plan, the attack, the splash, the tightening of the line, the run of the fish and the fight. No doubt about it, surface lure fishing was a sure-fire way to get the blood pumping. Sometimes the fish took the lure as soon as it hit the water, at other times when the lure was on the retrieve, and quite often (and most excitingly) right at the feet of the angler. Sometimes the fish didn't play the game, but that was fishing.

As Shrimp selected a surface lure manufactured to resemble a rat, he recalled a case which required him to think like a rat to lure his quarry.

A splash of rum in the pannikin of tea freshly poured from the billy, then settled for the night. Although not a loner, Daniel Nolan was a man more than content with his own company and his memories.

It was some of these memories that infiltrated his mind. Memories of his late wife, Maggie, and her sense of humour, her education, intelligence and her different way of seeing things. It was also memories of Sean Crosby and his unwitting nemesis, a Pacific Islander named Francis Aloa.

As a child, and to this day, the one thing Dan Nolan hated more than anything was to be called Danny Boy. He cringed each time he heard the song sung on the radio, at gatherings or spontaneous pub sing-a-longs.

Sean Crosby, he disliked intensely, not just for his criminality but for the fact that for years and years he was referred to by Crosby as Londonderry. Should they have passed on the street Crosby, in mock politeness, would tip his hat, or tug a forelock, and greet the policeman with, "Good morning, can't you just smell that Londonderry air," or, " Lovely afternoon, Detective Londonderry."

Shrimp knew it was an insult but could not work it out. It was one such greeting when he and Maggie were leaving the cinema that Sean Crosby, bowing low, uttered with a faux Irish lilt, "Ah! Mr. and Mrs. Nolan, tisn't it sweet to be a-breathin' the Londonderry air on the streets of Widenbridge? Did you enjoy the flick?"

Dan turned to Maggie inquiringly and said, "Crosby always calls me that and I just don't know why. I know it's a joke to him and the joke is on me, but I can't fathom it, Maggs."

Maggie smiled and then after a few paces along the footpath burst out in laughter that made the others on the street turn and stare. "Well, let me put it this way. Danny Boy, you hate. But through some quirk of music, at least from what I was taught by my school's piano teacher, Danny Boy is really only Danny Boy when sung. When played just as music, an instrumental, it is correctly titled Londonderry Air. What I think, and I'm sure I'm right in my interpretation, what Mr. Crosby is really calling you is London derrière which translates to him calling you, please pardon the language, Dan, the arsehole of London."

THE COFFEE CUP Cafe was as typical as any country town cafe. Apart from the hotels, mainly men's domain, the Coffee Cup, situated in Kurrajong Street, with a view of the Wombadgalong River, was a real social hub. Many a romance blossomed in the booths. Plans for functions and fundraising were hatched, witnessed by a teapot and a plate of scones. Posies in glass jars, decorated with a ribbon, were centred on the starched lace tablecloths laid with doilies. Two ceiling fans turned lazily in an effort to circulate a breeze. From the far end, above the chatter of the customers and the clinking of cutlery or crockery, was the cyclonic whirr of the milkshake maker. Couldn't the Coffee Cup Cafe make a milkshake? Any flavour, real ice-cream and milk only a degree or two above freezing served in a metal flute with a striped wax-paper straw. Two straws, if the drink was being shared. The mature ladies of the town preferred the tables near the door. There, the sunlight danced with the shadows of the rainbow-coloured entrance streamers on the polished timber floorboards. It all added to the natural warmth of the establishment. The young teenagers loved the booths. There they could, to the chagrin of the staff, stretch their legs on the cushioned seats and rest their elbows on the windowsill. Outside, Widenbridge went about its business.

Mrs. Woodford, proprietor, was a friendly woman on the exit side of middle age. She'd seen generations come and go. School children of all ages called in morning and afternoon for lollies, a packet of chewie, or a bag of chips. Every so often, on the pretext of community liaison, Detective Daniel Nolan would pop in and say "G'day". The real reason was most likely to buy a scorched peanut bar.

In was during one such visit that Mrs. Woodford invited the policeman beyond the curtain, into the kitchen, for a chat.

IT WAS EARLY third term and the students in their penultimate year at Widenbridge High School were excited about their pending work experience. This was their chance to sample real life. Life without blackboards, chalk, and homework. Some of the boys opted to work at one of the three service stations. One at the blacksmith behind the racecourse. One or two were disappointed that they weren't permitted by law, the school, or their parents to work at either the Jetty or Brigalow Hotels. Some of the girls attached themselves to the hospital, hoping to become nurses overnight. Others went to the banks, the solicitor's office, real estate or the vet. One student, Gail Milson, opted to spend her ten-day working assignment at the police station.

Gail Milson was a vibrant seventeen-year-old. She was loved by her parents and siblings. The girls and boys in her class at Widenbridge State High School voted her captain of their year debating team and she was elected one of the junior vice-captains of the school. Gail's teachers respected her work and her enquiring attitude. If she took risks, they were calculated. Her sharp mind and quick wit put her into and out of situations that would have others of her age, and older, scratching their heads. In short, Gail Milson had the world at her feet.

The many avenues of science twisted their way around Gail's brain. There was a career path she was seeking, but not yet finding. She was toying with criminology, hence the choice to do her work placement at the police station. As things worked out, Gail was passed from one department to the next. Insurance wouldn't permit her to be riding about with the highway crew. Widenbridge wasn't big enough to house a forensic team, let alone a laboratory. There was no arson squad. Such things, along with break and enter, robbery, serious assault, rape and murder, were handled by the small division of detectives.

What wasn't explained to the keen student was the amount of paperwork involved in policing. Nor were the periods of extended quiet, verging on boredom. She was soon to learn that when things happen it became exciting beyond the imagination, or due to vivid imagination.

Francis Aloa was a native of The New Hebrides. Through many twisted avenues in his life, he found himself a resident of Widenbridge. Most of his mates, including teammates of the Widenbridge Quolls rugby side, had no idea where The New Hebrides were. It was almost natural that through ignorance Francis became known, affectionately, as Fiji Frank or simply Fij.

He was a quiet man, but one with a sense of humour. After many a victory, during speeches, he would claim the win was due to the fact the Quolls boasted an All Black. This was a genesis for friendly banter, as all knew he certainly wasn't from New Zealand. Francis, at times, would like a little adventure in his existence. This would, if he was unlucky, lead him to appear before a visiting magistrate. His conduit to court from time to time was young Detective Daniel Nolan. The two were mates through football and various community activities, which both supported. Nolan often tried to counsel Francis, but couldn't quite bridge the cultural difference with often amusing results.

Fij Aloa was currently employed by a local farming family as a general hand. While work certainly wasn't foreign to him, grazing and cropping were. The farms that, for more than a century, flourished along the banks of the Wombadgalong River were structured and compartmentalised. Unlike his native islands, where families may or may not have taro patches. Any animals, mostly pigs and fowls, roamed freely. Fish were more than abundant and anyway, members of a tribe often dined together and shared village responsibilities on a socially balanced system.

It was while checking on some fencing along a stretch of river a mile or so from the homestead that the big man came across a patch of agriculture he'd never encountered before. What was strange was the fact this was in an area of dense bush. Access by river would be tricky. Detection from the main wheat paddocks was near impossible. Although the region was not in drought, it was heading in that direction. That's what caught Aloa's attention. This particular crop was lush and green. It was obviously well tended. As he worked his way to the fenceline running parallel to the river, he tripped. Looking down, he saw where some small native mammal had dug a burrow under a pipe that had been carefully buried to avoid detection.

Finding a solid branch laying on the ground, he traced the pipe to the river and found, very cleverly camouflaged by scrub, a small but powerful petrol pump, the exhaust system of which was wrapped in material designed to muffle as much noise as possible. That explained how the crop was watered, but what was it? Taking the pocket knife from the pouch on his belt, Francis pruned a little of the crop to take back to the house or into town to see if it could be identified.

Unbeknownst to Fiji Frank, a pair of eyes was watching from nearby. Those eyes didn't like what they were seeing. The brain behind the eyes was already calculating how to protect the crop. It wasn't just a crop to Crosby, it was cash.

***

Leading him as if he was a puppy, Mrs. Woodford ushered Detective Nolan into a small room beyond the activity of the cafe's kitchen.

"What's the problem, Mrs. Dub?" Dan wanted to know.

Wiping her hands on a floral apron, Mrs. Woodford sighed. "Mr. Nolan, it's those louts. You know the dirty looking layabouts who sit out front of the cafe? I know there's nothing wrong with anybody sitting there. They buy their snacks and something to drink, but I know they're up to no good. I'm not fond of smoking around food and children at the best of time, but those no-hopers just seem to spend their time rolling their smokes. Smoke after smoke they roll. Never seem to light them," she informed the detective.

"So!" Dan said, "if there's nothing wrong with them sitting there, what are they doing wrong?"

"That's just it, Detective. I really don't know. There does seem to be a lot of youngsters hanging about and then running or riding off fairly quickly. When I say youngsters, I mean both boys and girls from the high school. They don't come in, but I see plenty of wallets and purses being bought out of pockets. Plenty of sly looks, too. You know, looking to see if anyone can see what they're doing. Those kids know I'm not going to sell them any cigarettes. I'd be the first to let their parents know, but I think there is a trade in ready-rolled smokes happening right outside that front window. It's just a suspicion, mind you."

Dan ordered a sandwich and a cool drink, which he took to one of the tables outside the cafe. He stared at the table and the footpath. Nothing seemed out of place, nor did he expect things to be. As he brushed some crumbs away, a small speck caught his eye. Licking the top of his left index finger, he dabbed at the speck and lifted it to the light. Interesting! More examination showed similar specks caught in the creases where the chair seat melded with the back of the chair. Returning to the cafe, Dan asked for a small brush and a lolly bag. Carefully he brushed together what he could, then transferred the sweepings into the little white packet. "That'll head off to the lab down south this afternoon," he thought.

———

IN A FAR, dark corner of the Jetty Hotel, Sean Crosby and three of his associates were discussing matters nefarious in nature. Although he kept the location secret, Crosby informed the trio of a patch of weed in a near-inaccessible region bordered by the Wombadgalong River. He told them that his private garden was a source of income the members of the Australian Taxation Office need not know about. Impish giggles escaped from his audience. He also informed them that he had, at another location, enough "lawn clippings" to give the young and easily led of Widenbridge more than one good time. What was needed was help on the retail side of the business, help for which he would pay handsomely, help that those surrounding Sean Crosby would willingly give.

"I, gentlemen, have another problem. It concerns that bloody Aloa. He stumbled upon my little horticultural enterprise. I was there checking on my investment and there he was bumbling about. What should I do?" Crosby sarcastically asked of his audience. "He had the audacity to snip a sample. What for I don't know. The big oaf wouldn't know what to do with it. He needs to be taught a lesson, but who is going be the teacher?"

———

THE RESULTS from the lab came back. Apart from the expected detritus from a cafe environment, there was confirmation that what was collected contained an organic material identified as marijuana.

THE OLD UTE rattled along the dirt farm track that led to the road back to Widenbridge. Traffic was seldom a problem so far from town. Up ahead Francis Aloa could see a neighbouring farmer taking up the road with the tractor he was moving. The dust trail looked somewhat like a brown comet growing from the road. Not being in a hurry, he cruised gently, far enough behind the big machine as to not show impatience. Window down, elbow protruding from the car, Francis in his native tongue, sang a hymn well known in his islands. A tear, born of homesickness, escaped the corner of his eye. A smile seemed to split his face in two as a hearty laugh ejaculated from the depth of his soul. He realised what a sight he must have looked to anyone who could have been watching. Teeth as white as the purest thoughts were a contrast to his blue-black face as he happily sang in a rich, melodic baritone.

A pair of red-tailed black cockatoos lazily winged their slow-motion way over the vast wheat fields. Their strangled cries were loud enough to stop him mid song. His eyes tracked the birds as they flew towards the riverbank and the gumtree they called home. A second too late, he turned his attention back to the road. The tractor had slowed to a snail's pace as it arced across the road turning into a paddock. Hitting the brakes sent the ute into a skid that only stopped when it crashed into the rear wheel of the ag workhorse.

When he came to, Francis found himself laid out on the road. The flashing red light of the ambulance was the first thing he saw.

"Whoa, Big Fella," a gentle voice cautioned when he tried to sit up. "Let me help." The ambulance attendant and a uniformed policeman assisted him as he raised himself from the dusty road.

"Phew, eh brudda, what happened to the Fiji, eh?"

"Mr. Aloa, you and mister Deere, here, had a kissing competition, and you lost, my friend," replied the constable. "How are you feeling?"

"Eh, hey I tink I okay. Gees eh, that ute kinda bugga-up, eh? Dear oh dear, me boss not gonna like this one, or me, eh?"

"I wouldn't worry about your boss, mate, after what we found in the car, you'll have to worry more about what the judge has to say and I reckon he'll be pretty cranky.

"START AGAIN, PLEASE."

"Well, Dan-"

"Hang on Frank, in here it's Detective or Mr. Nolan, understand? That's how it is, okay?"

"Kay' Dan, ah Mister Nolan. Well, like I say to you eh, I was workin' way back paddock b'long Mr. Ogden an I see this one place all green. 'What's this Fij, eh?' I say to me and I go look, see. I walkin' along this place when bugga me, Dan, ah sorry, Mr. Detective, I kick somefink. Lookin' down eh I see em big irrigation pipe. It goes inta the river. I don' know this crop. Cut a bit off to show Mr. Ogden or that Jess at Agriculture 'Pardment. Better probably Jess, what you reckon Dan, eh?"

"Fair dinkum Frank! This stuff is illegal. I believe you, mate, but you've got me stumped. Tell you what, I'll get hold of an unmarked car and one of the back-room boys to run us both out there and you show me."

News filtered to Sean Crosby that Francis Aloa had stacked his ute and he was arrested for having a quantity of marijuana in his possession. Crosby smiled; the gods were looking over him.

Checking on the pump and reorganising the camouflage, Crosby heard chatter from up in the paddock. Silently, he made his way some distance from the pump and the voices. Peering through natural scrub, he could make out the big islander and that copper, Nolan. Crosby cursed to himself.

Francis Aloa reached out and grabbed Shrimp by the shoulder. His eyes widened as he opened his mouth to speak. In an attempt to walk away, Dan Nolan, deliberately, stood on the left instep of the big man who uttered a cry of surprise then, by way of reflex, pushed the policeman over. Straight away, he apologised and went to help Dan to his feet.

"Thanks, Fij'. I knew you'd do that. I saw him, too. I just didn't want you to tell me in case he heard. We have to let him think we haven't spotted him. Don't even look that way. Come on, back to the car."

Before leaving the cafe, Shrimp had requested Mrs. Woodford inform him when the 'cigarette rollers' were plying their trade outside her establishment. It wasn't long before she rang.

Walking into the Coffee Cup Detective Nolan ignored what was happening at the footpath tables. Inside, he ordered a sandwich. Outside, serendipity played a hand. Unknown to the policeman, Sean Crosby took a seat outside the cafe. Dan's colleagues were waiting for him to come outside. As he stepped from the doorway, he noticed Crosby with a package in his hand. When he saw his adversary, he tried to palm the packet to one of the louts at the table, who was too dumbfounded at seeing Shrimp to take the parcel from his cohort.

"Good afternoon, Mr. Crosby. What do you have there?"

Crosby kicked his chair away but as he turned to run, he hit a wall of khaki uniform. Dan took the parcel. Crosby took on a pair of handcuffs. As he was led away, he gave a nod to one of the boys at the table and said, "Tell Promise."

Forty-five minutes later, still in handcuffs, Sean Crosby sat opposite Detective Daniel Nolan inside the Widenbridge Police Station. Although the packet of marijuana and its owner were in custody, Shrimp had an uneasy feeling. Questions were asked. The only answer was an arrogant smirk.

The police station at Widenbridge was not a big building. The cells at the back were secure enough to hold prisoners in a small degree of dignity before either being transferred to a larger centre or released. The amenities, two cubicles each for the female and male staff, were at the rear of the detectives' offices. It was to these cubicles that a uniformed officer made his way. Less than ninety seconds later, he was occupying himself near some filing cabinets.

"Whatcha think ya gunna do with me, Londonderry?" Crosby smugly asked.

Before Dan could answer, a small explosion echoed from the toilets. About eight seconds later, there was another. Instinctively Dan put the packet of drugs in his top drawer, then with most of the others in the office, ran to where the drama had unfolded.

Gail Minson remained quiet in a corner of the office. She said nothing but noticed much. Acting like he belonged, a young uniformed police officer went to Dan Nolan's desk and salvaged the evidence. Holding it up, he spoke softly to Crosby then left the building.

Fifteen minutes after the explosions, Dan returned. There was no real damage to the men's room, but the place was littered with red and charred paper and an aroma usually associated with Guy Fawkes night. The diversion was an old but simple schoolboy prank. The only things needed to pull it off were, in this case, two tailor made cigarettes and some twopenny bungers. The cigarettes were lit. Small holes were made a little just above the filter tip to take the wick of the fireworks and the crude bang-bang was ready. By the time the cigarette had burned away enough to reach and ignite the wicks, the perpetrator could be well away.

"Sean!" Crosby looked up. "I can't help but think you were behind this."

"Oh c'mon Mr. Nolan, I was handcuffed here the whole time. Anyway, waddaya gunna charge me with?"

"For a start, my friend," Dan opened his drawer. An expletive softly escaped. "Wwwhaat have you done with it, Crosby?"

"Done with what, sir?" was the smiling reply.

Reaching for his key ring, Shrimp uncuffed his prisoner and told him to get out. He also issued a warning that this incident was far from over. After Crosby had left, Gail Milson approached Dan. She mentioned to Shrimp the young policeman who took the package from the desk drawer. Her description was of a youngish man, with a day or two of stubble which looked out of place on an officer. He had sergeant's stripes but no chrome numbers on his lapels. She said he also walked without discipline. Gail mentioned that with an air of confidence, the mysterious policeman took the parcel from the top draw and said, "Detective Nolan told me to keep this safe." To himself, Dan cursed. The station sergeant had been with him out the back, following the explosions.

IN THE DARK, a kookaburra sang his pre-dawn song. It was enough to rouse Shrimp from his slumber. Stretching in his swag, he turned to the east to see the first hint of daylight, the piccaninny dawn. Making his way to the embers of last night's fire, he added twigs. Once they caught, heavier wood was fed to the flames. He filled his billy and went for a walk to chase the sleep from his bones. He liked not having to shave. He liked not having to dress to impress somebody. He loved the early morning bush.

A cup of tea and some toast was all he needed to get going. Rod in hand, he made his way to the river. Adjusting the reel to the weight of the lure, he made the first of many casts for the day. It didn't happen often, but as that cast hit the water, the fish hit the lure. He was unprepared for the sudden action. The line peeled from the reel as it cut through the water as a scythe cuts through barley at an Amish harvest.

Adrenaline coursed through his bloodstream. His breathing became intense and the muscles in his arms, yet to be warm, protested. For Shrimp Nolan, this was Utopia, Shangri-la and Nirvana rolled up together and delivered at his feet.

It was a decent fish. The fight it put up was a worthy match for the old fellow. Slowly, instinctively calling on the experience of many such a fight, Dan turned the tiring creature and attempted to bring it to the bank. Giving the effect of roller-skates, loose pebbles under his feet almost caused him to lose balance. Somewhere high behind him, the kookaburra again tilted its head back over its shoulders and, with beak wide open, laughed loudly.

"Cheeky bugger" thought Dan. He'd forgotten his landing net and, like the jackass, gave forth with a long, hearty laugh.

With a flick of paddle tail, the fish was free of the lure. Rolling slightly to its right, it seemed to look the angler in the eye as if to say, "Till next time, friend," before lazily swimming back to the log it called home. Thinking back, Shrimp realised this wasn't the first fish he'd hooked that had outsmarted him.

"Mr. Nolan, what do you do now? Surely you just can't let him go?" Gail asked.

"That's all I can do, Gail. Without evidence, well... anyway there are two positives to come out of this. One, Mr. Crosby will slip up again. Two, lose a fish or, in this case, a criminal, sit and think of where one went wrong, then don't let it happen again. I'll just have to outthink him next time we meet. Wait here, please Gail."

Shrimp went into an adjoining office, then returned with four thick photo albums. "Righto, my girl, let's see if you can find the mystery policeman."

Leaning back in his chair, Dan and Gail discussed her school life. He turned the conversation to the use of drugs by the students. She said that maybe half a dozen of the kids who were troublemakers would probably be into it. There was playground talk, of course. Gossip more than anything, but she wouldn't be surprised.

"Yes, you would be Gail. Yes, you would be surprised."

Visiting his local tackle shop, Dan was introduced to the world of lures by the visiting salesman.

"What! These things catch fish?" was his reaction.

The salesman offered two of the lures to Dan to try. Each had two sets of treble hooks hanging from them. One was black and purple. As for the other one, it was lime green with white stripes. Both were basically fish shaped, both had some silly kind of protruding bib with an eyelet to attach the fishing line, and both had a flash of red under the chin. Dan thanked the salesman but said he'd pay for them. He wished he hadn't. They were expensive.

After he was shown how to tie the lures to his line, he was given a demonstration on how to cast them. It took a little time before he caught onto the idea. Later that afternoon after work, he went to the local park to practise with his new toys. Young Lonnie Quinn walked up to him and asked if he'd caught any.

"You're the fifth, Lonnie."

Both laughed.

It took hours and hours of casting till eventually Dan could be so accurate he could put the lure within six inches of the intended target. He found that the lures did catch fish, and he soon added to the number. No more than a year after the salesman sold him his first two lures, Dan was no longer fishing with bait. It had been said that lures were designed to catch fishermen, not fish. Detective Daniel Nolan of the Widenbridge Constabulary was hooked.

So it seemed that more and more of the Widenbridge youth were being hooked and it wasn't on fishing. Mrs. Woodford was ecstatic that the front of her cafe was no longer the hangout of local louts.

Word got about. The manager of the local cinema mentioned to someone that the kids were becoming somewhat cheekier. Sports coaches noticed numbers had dropped off, and teachers came to the realisation that some of their brightest students had dropped in grades and three or four of them had dropped classes. Teachers and parents were so concerned that they organised meetings with town leaders and authorities.

It was at one such meeting that Detective Daniel Nolan found himself the target of passionately irate parents. As with any small community, rumours and innuendo were passed along quicker than a summer cold in a boardingschool dormitory. Some were quick to target Francis Aloa, as they'd heard he had been cultivating marijuana and was on his way into Widenbridge with his harvest when he crashed his ute. Others 'knew' he was selling the drug to their children. Tempers flared and accusations were aimed at Detective Nolan, claiming he, being a mate of that big native bastard, was in with him and probably making a fair whack on top of his handsome police pay. As Dan rose to defend the erroneous claim, a strong voice rose too, one that required anyone who heard it pay attention. The voice belonged to Peter Minson.

The dark mood of the meeting lightened somewhat when Peter Minson explained his daughter was witness to the fact an alleged perpetrator, not Francis Aloa, was for a brief time in custody. He placated the crowd by saying that at the time of the minor explosions at the police station, as reported in the Widenbridge Word newspaper, the suspect was being interviewed by Detective Nolan.

There were two teenagers, easily led girls who were part of Crosby's network, attending the meeting. They kept quiet at the back of the auditorium. No one noticed them, or the fact they were taking notes. The girls and the notes soon found themselves in the company of Sean Crosby.

FOOTBALL CLUBS ATTRACTED all kinds of people who, themselves, were attracted to the sport for all kinds of reasons. There were those who had a strong compunction to be associated with others in a team situation, those who loved the physical aspect of the game. Others found the science and structure of the contest a fascination, while some just enjoyed knocking about and knocking the opposition about while trying not to be too knocked about in the process.

The Widenbridge Quolls happened to be a tight outfit. Not just the senior team, but the lower grades right down to the seven- and eight-year-old boys learning the game. The Quolls trained twice a week pre-season and during the home and away competition. Should they find themselves in the finals, they upped the regime to three times a week. Tuesday nights, the club trained as a whole unit. Thursday nights, the first and second grade squads trained together while the lower grade coaches took their charges through their own routines. As a referee, and in order to keep his own fitness level up, Dan Nolan trained with the local teams, the Quolls, and at times, the Daneborough Vikings. This gave the players a positive rapport with the man controlling the game, whilst at the same time gave Shrimp, as a ref, the chance to know the players and the style of footy they played.

One particular Tuesday night, while at training, one of the under-fifteen lads asked Shrimp if he could talk to him. It transpired that the lad's cousin was a break-away for the Vikings. He told Shrimp that some of his cousin's teammates were involved in smoking weed. The story was some bloke from Widenbridge was offering the stuff around. Seems the fellow was hunting down one of the Viking forwards to make an impression on a certain Pacific Islander. It wasn't a friendly gesture being offered. The word was that Sean Crosby was offering the forward, a chap who had a reputation of violence, on and off the field, a sum of cash and a supply of marijuana to do serious damage to Francis Aloa. Serious enough to put the big islander in hospital and serious enough to finish Frank's footy, if not working, career. Shrimp thanked the boy and told him not to mention the situation to anyone and not to say he'd been speaking to him.

After training, Dan invited Frank over for a drink. "Gees, Dan, eh you know I not be on the drink during the season, but hey, what is it you wantin'?"

Shrimp told him the story. "Ooh! Whatcha reckon we do 'bout it, eh? We tell the boys and turn it on and take dat bloke outa the match."

"No," said Dan, "don't you do anything, just leave it to me."

THE FEW ARTICLES pertaining to freshwater angling that Shrimp could get his hands on were studied with relish. Notes were made and theories, offered by the readings, put into practice. One thing that was emphasised in many articles was that native fish were ambush feeders and would lie in wait by a large rock or submerged log waiting for prey. Structure! That's what the experts called it. The fish were, more often than not, found where there was structure in the water. Dan was soon looking for trees that had fallen into the river or the tip of a boulder that protruded above the waterline. Casting his lures to such a structure started to pay. As with many aspects of fishing and crime fighting, Dan knew that patience was key.

One did not just walk to a river bank and accurately cast a

lure. It took many hours, over many weeks, of learning how to put a lure in the right spot. Dan did this by setting up half a dozen jam tins at different distances and casting a hookless lure as close as possible to his makeshift targets. His endeavour was to land the lure in the tins. It took time to understand the way the weight of the lure took it through the air. It took technique to adapt to different wind speed and direction. It took dedication and when it came to fishing, Shrimp Nolan had dedication in bus loads.

THE COLOURS of autumn decorated the surrounds of the beer garden at the rear of the Jetty Hotel. Rust-coloured leaves fluttered as they fell from the grapevines growing over the pergola. The ornamental pear trees added shades of fading green and sun-bright yellow to the palette of the season. Looking out of place, a hedge of rosemary gave an uncharacteristic sense of formality in a rather casual setting.

Looking quite informal was the group of drinkers in the far corner of the beer garden. Holding court was Sean Crosby. Beer schooners, in various stages of consumption, adorned the lopsided, scalloped edged, circular tin table with faded and chipped paint. The ashtray in the table's centre was near to overflowing with dog ends. The drinkers leaned towards the man telling his story. To anyone eavesdropping as Crosby spoke, it could be as if they were listening to one of those Sunday night radio preachers presenting a spiel. "It is nature that begat the earth; the earth begat the soil; the soil begat the nutrients, and the nutrients fed the seeds."

He continued, "The seeds begat the seedlings; the seedlings begat the plant; the plant begat the leaves; the leaves begat the crop; the crop begat the supply; the supply begat the demand; the demand begat by the users; the users begat the cash, and the cash begat much happiness within me."

When he finished his parody from the First Book of Chronicles, Sean Crosby took a draught from his glass. Looking over the rim, he could see that his sycophantic audience was impressed by his speech. He also knew that none of them was capable of understanding his little Biblical joke.

"That cash of which I spoke, gentlemen, I am now prepared to divide between you." Crosby returned to a Biblical scenario. It amused him, but again he knew it was above those gathered about. "I shall send you out, two by two, into the streets and the neighbouring towns to spread the word. That word is 'grass'. Take not with you identification, for the law may find wont to descend upon you. Spread the good news that high times are to be had. Give freely in the first instance, for surely, I say to you, there will be instances of the second, third, fourth and beyond for which the seekers will gladly pay. Return to me and then receive your reward. I do not send you so that you may speak of me. No! You must not speak of me to those with whom you do commerce. I strictly forbid you to do so. No! Do not utter my name to any man of police. I know you, but when trouble comes, as trouble may well come, you do not know me."

It wasn't long before the region was deluged by a green storm.

As she walked home from school on a cool Thursday afternoon in late May, Gail Minson planned to make a stop at the Widenbridge Library. Lounging on a park bench in the late autumn sun was a man in his mid-twenties. A lock of unwashed blonde hair fell lazily over his right eye. He gave the appearance of being unemployed and up to no good. Technically that would not have been correct. Although he held no position of employment, he was on the payroll of Sean Crosby. That in itself was confirmation of him being up to no good.

"Um, 'scuse me love, you woulden' av a sec would ya?"

Gail was about to ignore him and continue on her quest, but an instinct caused her to stop and talk to the man. It took a few seconds before she recognised him. She expected a sleazy pick-up line, but that didn't come. What he did say shocked her, as she didn't expect such a proposal. Would she like an ounce of good times? Just a little something that will make the pressure of exams ease. "Won't cost ya nuffin' to try, promise ya," was the clincher.

Gail sat in a modest pose next to the man. "What do I do with it? How does it work?" she asked in feigned innocence.

He explained. A packet of cigarette papers was attached to a small wad by a rubber band. The man tucked the tiny package into Gail's school satchel.

"That should last ya a little while. When ya want some more good times, I can deliver 'em to ya, here, next Furzdee. This lot is a free sample, but you'd need to pay next time. Its gunna be wurf it, promise ya."

Gail smiled, thanked him and said maybe next Thursday might be alright. The man smiled, stood to go and said, "Hey listen love, you tell ya friends, there's plenty for everybody, promise ya."

"Yes, I'll do that," said Gail.

He watched as she made her way to the library. There was something ticking at the back of his brain. It kept itself hidden enough that he couldn't retrieve it. Whatever it was faded away as he gave a brief wave to his mate working the other side of the park.

A couple of young lads were kicking a football along the path between some trees. "Hey, you blokes, you wanna bag fulla good times? Better than footy, promise ya."

DAPPLED SHADOWS DANCED over Dan Nolan's camping gear. A wisp of smoke rose from the campfire ashes. Crows and cockatoos cawed and screeched as if battling for supremacy of the bush. Ducks with wings spread wide and legs extended gently skied to a stop on the river. Honeyeaters and small birds chasing insects fluttered in and around the riparian foliage.

There were many theories about catching fish, Shrimp mused. Come to that there were many theories about catching criminals. Fish, he was sure, didn't ponder the prospects of falling to a bait or a lure. On the other hand, criminals, he was sure, didn't ponder getting caught by the police.

As he checked and, where necessary, retied lines, Shrimp let his thoughts go back to the Crosby case. He thought how at the time even soft drugs were not a part of the culture of the Widenbridge youth. It was Francis Aloa who, unwittingly, was the trigger for that scum Crosby coming undone. It took time, and it took unorthodox methods. Shrimp recalled how ironic it was that while Crosby was getting the kids of the region hooked, he, Crosby, was to be hooked by the law.

DISGUISED as farm workers or dressed in army surplus camouflage outfits members of both the Widenbridge and

Daneborough constabularies were spending their days watching a patch of wilting green crop on the banks of the Wombadgalong River. The pump used to water the crop had been engineered to falter due to a clever electric timer surreptitiously wired into the works. The crop was flagging.

Unknown to him, the eyes of the law were boring into the back of Sean Crosby as he inspected his enterprise. Shaking his head as he tried to work out what was happening, he made his way down the river bank to inspect his pump. Nearby a constable froze and held his breath as his falling foot snapped a dead branch. Crosby also stopped and dropped to one knee. His eyes widened as he scanned his surrounds. A smile almost broke out as, looking in the direction of the noise, he saw a pair of echidnas scurrying along their way. Out of frustration he went to kick one of the animals but quickly changed his mind. He knew what those spines could do to a foot.

THE RIVALRY between the Quolls and the Vikings dates back beyond anyone's recollection. Fierce games, tough games, games that were won by the narrowest margin, to blow-out score lines favouring either side. It wasn't war when the whistle blew but, it wasn't far from it.

This particular Saturday afternoon was perfect for playing rugby. A lazy zephyr gave neither team an advantage. The sun radiated a temperature conducive to hard, physical sport. In the distance, the low ranges were clear in view.

Most of those attending the game gathered on the western side of the ground. Many of the women, among them, girlfriends and wives of the players found their regular place in the stands. Others, the men and players from the lower grades gathered in groups adjacent to the clubhouse entrance. This gave them both a view of the game and easy access to the bar. At either end of the field the first-grade sides went through their final workouts and warm-ups. Most were expecting a hard, fast, but fair, contest.

The Daneborough Vikings travelled to the Widenbridge Memorial Sports Ground, the Mem, in their club bus. The coach and the captain discussed tactics. As it should be with any team, the various members had input. There was one, though, who had a secondary agenda. Preston Baines was one of the front row forwards. As it was, his drop in performance of recent times, coupled with a waning of dedication at training, saw him relegated to the bench. Personal plans were unravelling. It was during the warm up he had his opportunity to rectify his situation. Positioning himself by a fellow forward he leapt to take a high ball. The landing looked innocent enough though the resulting broken collarbone put the selected player out and Baines in.

At three fifteen the two teams, the match officials, and the ball boys made their way onto the ground. The national anthem played followed by the Quoll's club song.

Asking both captains if they were ready and with a point to the timekeeper and scorers, referee Nolan raised his right arm and blew his whistle. The game was underway.

By the eastern boundary fence a lone spectator watched on. His focus was not on the game as such, but on two particular players. Crosby was not one hundred percent sure that Baines could do what he was being paid to do. Francis Aloa knew he was a target, but didn't know whose target he was. Having witnessed the incident prior to the game, Dan was positive he'd have to watch Baines.

Fights in football games had differing affects. For the crowd they provided much entertainment. The players found a blue a good way to release pent up sporting emotion. As for the referee, it gave him the chance to either stamp his authority on the game or lose control of it.

Dan noticed that Baines seemed to be marking Aloa. When the ball cleared a ruck and the big forward took it up, Baines made straight for him. Of course it may well be a part of the defensive structure of the Vikings game. But when Francis dropped back to catch his breath and view the state of play, Dan noticed Baines stalking his man.

The first scrum of the game was fed by the Daneborough side. Baines needed to concentrate in helping to push the Quolls off the ball. After all, he was there as a member of a team trying to win.

Dan had his plan to save Francis from getting hurt. He figured a repeat of the episode out at the farm would do the trick. He didn't get a chance to find out. An indiscretion by the Vikings saw the setting of another scrum, this time with the loose head and feed to Widenbridge. As the packs came together an arm that wasn't gripping the jersey of the man next to it swung from near grass level to glance off the sweaty cheek of Francis Aloa. Simultaneously there were an explosion of bodies and a roar of anger loud enough to put the few birds perched on the goalpost crossbar to flight. The crowd cheered as one. They had no idea what the trigger was, but an all-in melee was always worth the price of admission.

On the eastern boundary Crosby shook his head in disbelief. On the field one man was fuelled with fury, another was filled with fear. Baines had a job to do. He had a target to hit, he missed. Aloa was unstoppable. Rugby was a gentleman's game. Hard, rough and uncompromising, but a gentleman's game, nonetheless. Unsolicited violence was taboo. Reaching out a hand that was capable of crushing a crab in its shell, Francis clasped his spread-eagled fingers around Baines' face and lifted him half his body height and threw him like a crumpled sandwich wrapper onto the ground. Other players were involved in their own little scraps. The referee's whistle was blowing overtime.

Baines, winded from the attack from Aloa, was slow to rise. Francis was onto his man in about three paces. It was then that Dan came between the big man from the New Hebrides and the thug from Daneborough. It took seven of Francis' team mates to hold him back.

Before Dan could lay down the law, Baines scowled at Aloa and said, "This isn't over, friend." The fire in the big native's eyes should've been a warning but Baines never saw it.

"Yes, it am!" said Fiji Frank as he let fly with a right hand that broke the jaw of the opposition forward.

With that Dan confronted the big fellow with whistle blazing. "You're gone Aloa, take a shower."

Francis Aloa stormed off the field. Baines was taken to the local hospital where arrangements for transfer to the city for surgery were made. Crosby was not a happy man.

GAIL MINSON KNEW she was taking a risk in accepting the packet of marijuana. She even suspected she was breaking the law. There were no doubts, in Gail's mind, that the man who was peddling the substance was the same fellow who removed the evidence from Detective Nolan's desk.

"Dad! don't touch it. We'll take it down to the police station and show Detective Nolan. I haven't touched it. The only fingerprints on it would belong to that man from the park."

"You should've come to me straight away, Gail. Possession

is as much a crime as growing or selling. How much did this cost you?" Shrimp inquired.

"Not a thing, Mr. Nolan, but he did say next time I'll have to pay."

"Next time?"

"Yes, on Thursday at the park opposite the library."

"Well then," said Dan, "you better not disappoint him. If that's okay with you Peter?"

"If it helps to put these parasites behind bars and if you can guarantee Gail's safety, then yes, if Gail is alright with it."

"Dad, of course I'm alright with it. This is policing. This is a real taste of what I want to do."

AROUND THE CLOCK observation posts were manned at the farm. Lack of water and a dose of selected herbicide put the crop into decline. The decision was made to watch and by clandestine methods sabotage the drug growing enterprise.

Dan Nolan was always a hands-on policeman. Whenever he organised a case, he was involved at each level. It was while he was checking the riverbank upstream of the farm, he found a small aluminium boat hidden in the scrub. Without disturbing the hiding place he reached into the stern and removed the bung. There was no doubt that the boat belonged to Crosby. Small scraps of marijuana littered the boat's floor.

Years of police work had sharpened Shrimp's instincts. He knew things were coming to a head. The only sticking point was where Crosby had stored the harvested crop. Patience was the key.

THURSDAY, at school, Gail was tense with excitement. She threw herself into her schoolwork and studies. Both little lunch and big lunch were an annoyance as she was keen to be at the park playing her 'undercover' role. Three o'clock came soon enough. Gail told her friends she needed to go to the library.

The park bench was vacant. Red, gold and brown autumn leaves were picked up in a little willie-willie. A magpie swooped on some unsuspecting insect. In the distance, young mothers with their toddlers played on the swings and roundabout. Anticipation permeated the atmosphere.

Sitting on the bench Gail read a school textbook. In her peripheral vision she noticed a pair of jean-clad legs next to her. Before she could look up a voice said, "Promised cha I'd be here. Did ya have a high old time of it? Promised cha ya would. Now what I got here is even better but it'll cost ya."

Promise was too wrapped up in his spiel to notice there was someone behind him. As he went to put the package into Gail's satchel, he felt a cold clasp on his wrist as a handcuff was applied with swift dexterity. Across the way a young man noticed what was happening and started to run. A constable in plain clothes put an end to his flight.

At Widenbridge Police Station, the two pushers were left alone in the closed interview room. "What's gunna happen to us, Promise?" the young man asked.

"Promise ya mate the Croz will get us out. We done lots a stuff for him. He won't let us down, just don't mention his name to the cops."

"Mention whose name?" asked detective Nolan as he entered the room. Before he could think Promise started to say Crosby and then stopped himself. Then with an air of self-confidence said "Cro... Crowly, that's him, that's whose name it was."

"So this Crowly is the mastermind, is it?" Dan asked.

"Yeh, Crowley."

"Bill Crowley, Tom Crowley, Colin Crowley? Which Crowley?"

"Nuh, none of them Crowleys."

"Well which Crowley is it?"

"You guess, copper."

The conversation, at Dan's instigation, picked up pace. "Tim Crowley?"

"No!"

"Gary Crowley?"

"Nuh."

"Pat Crowley, Jim Crowley, Clive Cowley?"

Promise was enjoying the guessing game and answered the questions as quickly as they were fired at him. "No, no, no."

"Trevor Crowley?"

"No."

"Sean Crosby?"

"Yeh, at last, um no, no, not Sean Crosby."

"Gotcha," said Dan.

"Go home, go home! That's all he said Maggs, go home."

"Dan, I'm sure Superintendent Patterson had his reasons. You stopped the street sellers. That's a good thing. You thought there may have been more than two. Your investigation nabbed eight. That's a win, darl."

"No Maggie, it's points, but it's not a win. Without Crosby there is no win and Crosby has disappeared from the planet. Vanished. We cleaned up the crop. No Crosby. We took eight scums out of business. No Crosby. Francis may face deportation, thanks to Crosby. Mind you, I don't think Baines will play, or want to play, rugby again, plus he faces an assault charge for breaking that bloke's collarbone. Crosby has much to answer. The one shining light was Gail. She stayed out of the way during that fire cracker fiasco, but showed the wherewithal to notice Crosby's underling. Even though she couldn't find his picture in the mug shot albums, it was smart of her to recognise him as the same bloke who turned out to be her dealer. Still, no Crosby."

A knock at the door interrupted their conversation. Dan heard Maggie invite the visitors inside. "Comb your hair Daniel, there are people here to see you."

Moving into the living room Shrimp was greeted by Peter and Gail Minson. "What an honour to have the heroine of Widenbridge grace our humble abode," said Dan, "and with a chaperone."

Gail blushed a little and Peter held up two large bottles of beer.

"Every man has his price." Dan smiled. Before the men retired to the back porch, it was decided that the ladies, Maggie and Gail, should collect Gail's mum, some supplies from the butcher and green grocer and then the men would light the barbecue.

"Crosby was a mongrel at school, Shrimp, and he's a mongrel now. I'm lucky to have a girl with a smart head on her shoulders. Poor Gail, she's not too popular with a few of the kids, but she's done the right thing. Patty and I are more than proud of her. Thank you, mate, for watching over her."

Monday morning was always a rush at the police station: weekend traffic offences to process, minor criminal reports to follow up and, for the detectives, briefings to attend.

Superintendent Patterson, 'Curse' behind his back, informed the team of a possible sighting of Sean Crosby. Dan straightened in his chair. It transpired that some bush walkers stumbled across a rough set up on the river some distance from town. Nothing unusual, they thought, until they received a hostile reception. Their friendly salutations were rebuked strongly, and it was made clear their presence was not welcomed. The reaction by the scruffy hermit was enough to set a worry in the walkers so they reported their concerns to the police.

"Nolan, your case, your call," came from the Super.

"I'd like five men, sir, with walkie-talkies. I'll pose as a fisherman,"

"You always pose as a fisherman, Nolan," was an utterance from the back.

Giggles rippled through the meeting.

"I'll do what I try to do best, catch criminals and fish. It's been suggested that, in theory, a whale can be landed by using a reel of cotton. There's no reason to call me Ishmael, but Crosby is my whale."

The cars were left some distance either side of the camp. Dan's instructions to the five officers were basic. Wait twenty minutes while he set up his fishing spot. When the time came to move in, they were to do it in such a fashion as to alert Crosby. They must banter on the walkie-talkies and move into positions as if trying not to be seen.

On the riverbank Shrimp wished he really was fishing. The Wombadgalong flowed steadily on it journey as it probably had done since time began. Normally he would have found great delight in watching the two platypuses work their stretch of water. A gum bough, laden with spent flower nuts, kissed the stream. Wood swallows danced an aerial ballet. All this while Dan tied a lure to his line. Dressed in a ragged pair of dungarees, an old flannel shirt with one sleeve missing and a hat that hid his facial features, Detective Nolan looked anything but the law officer he was.

Wearing an earpiece Dan monitored the operation the five others were putting into effect. As he hoped the action by the 'bungling' uniform boys worked. It wasn't long before a figure, constantly looking over his shoulder, broke into the clearing and onto the river flat.

"G'day digger, you got a bull chasin' ya?" Dan said.

Startled, Crosby stopped to see where the voice came from. An angry grunt was the reply. Dan, unobtrusively lifted his fishing rod and prepared to cast. Crosby stopped briefly, without recognition, looked at the angler and hurried on.

When Crosby was some twenty paces along Dan called out, "Crosby, you're under arrest, stop!"

Sean Crosby exclaimed, "Nolan! Like hell, you never caught me yet and you aren't going to catch me now." With that he turned to run. Hardly had he moved when what he thought was a branch hit his neck and a wasp applied its sting. Reaching back to swat the offending insect his hand exploded in a swarm of painful bites. Dan set the lure. With his right hand over his left shoulder, Crosby could do little but stagger. The pain of four of six needle sharp treble hooks imbedded past the barbs into the palm of the drug dealer's hand was agony. The more he pulled, the more tension Dan applied to the line. Almost whimpering, with blood streaming along his arm and dripping from his elbow, Sean Crosby fell to his knees. A familiar tune filled the felon's ears. As Detective Daniel Nolan, Widenbridge Police, wound in his line while softly whistled Londonderry Air.

A CRESCENT MOON rode high in the night sky. Treetops swayed gently, as if fanning the ground. High in the branches, nocturnal creatures scratched the timber as they played and hunted in the canopy. At ground level, cicadas emerged from their subterranean abodes.

Sitting on a low stool, Shrimp Nolan, detective, retired, used an old metal spatula with a melted groove in its plastic handle to flip the two fillets of a fish that less than an hour ago was unaware that a predator, was about to strike. That was nature. Big fish hunted little fish. Bigger fish hunted the next size down and somewhere there was something or someone to hunt the bigger fish.

On the banks of the Wombadgalong River Shrimp let the people of that case from so long ago visit his memories. Mrs. Woodford had long ago passed on. Peter and Patty Minson retired to a quiet village on the coast. Gail Minson never studied criminology; she was now a project manager on an oil rig in the Indian Ocean. Promise, who knew? Maggie, well not a day or even an hour went by when she wasn't in his thoughts. Crosby? That nemesis fell foul playing some scheme behind bars. Shrimp wondered why he recalled that particular case. As he spread a slice of damper with butter a distant, haunting howl rode the night breeze.

THE END

THE LEMON TREE

The wipers were working overtime on the old ute. Just before the storm started delivering rain in javelin like shafts and hail the size of a man's big toenail, Shrimp Nolan had stowed his fishing gear in the tray. Securing the tonneau cover, just in time, he drove to a clearing adjacent to the riverbank in order to avoid falling branches. Lightning danced above the treetops. To Shrimp, it was like he was trapped in a eucalyptus faraday cage.

The storm had interrupted a good morning's fishing. From just after dawn, Shrimp had been fervently casting lures into the waters of the Wombadgalong River. The morning was still. Still and quiet. The only noise was the sound of Shrimp's lures striking the water surface. Not a bird sang. Not an insect buzzed or chirped. Usually ducks worked that stretch of water. It was not unusual to see a platypus or two searching for a meal of worms or crustaceans. Not today! Leaves hung limp on low branches. The humidity was high, and the air was thick. Shrimp guessed the barometric pressure was dropping. Still, without warning, a fish ambushed his lure. There was a theory that fish will 'go on the bite' when there was a dramatic change in the weather, such as a sudden storm.

Two nice native specimens, a little larger than pan size, now occupied a bucket in the back of the ute. Experience, both as an angler and a detective, had taught him to always be aware. The sky that was so clear when he arrived soon started to collect cloud. Not the blanket nimbus that heralded showers. No, these clouds were pillars that climbed into the heavens. Clouds that grew and boiled. With each roll-over they became larger and more threatening. Experience had taught him that storms that build rapidly were potentially violent. At first, it was a distant rumble, easy enough to ignore. Soon that rumble became an orchestral percussion section. It was then that a breeze created wavelets on the water. The birds, so quiet before, flew en masse upstream away from the approaching tempest.

That was enough for Shrimp. With careful haste, he put what he could into the ute and covered it. He drove to the clearing. It was as if there was a switch thrown. Day became almost night. A pea-soup green tinted the cloud. The rain was not just heavy, it was a deluge. Shrimp knew it was pointless to drive back to Widenbridge. Visibility was no more than two feet at the optimistic most. No, he'd just have to sit this one out. The wind seemed to gust, without discipline, from all points of the compass simultaneously.

Peering through the windscreen, Shrimp could see the canopy dancing an unchoreographed ballet. Leaves let go of their stems, stripping branches bare. Sheets of bark twisted in his vision. Behind the ute a massive bough crashed to the ground.

"The old man always told us never to go to trees for shelter in a storm." Shrimp mused to himself. "Glad I listened to him," he mumbled.

Eventually, the storm abated. Drizzle persisted adding moisture to the saturated leaf littered flat. Winding down his window, Shrimp noticed how destructive the storm had been. Leaves spun without resistance in puddles being fed by streamlets meandering towards the river. Branches that would soon make homes for small mammals or little reptiles, now rested by the trees that sprouted them as twigs years, if not decades, earlier. The temptation to return to fishing was strong, but common sense ruled and he decided to return home. The two fish in the tray of the ute would be more than an adequate meal.

Nature had always infatuated Daniel Nolan. The passing of the seasons, the times of drought and of flooding. The starry firmament. The nature of the criminal mind, which was why he became a policeman. He marvelled at the storm that grew from nothing. The storm that vented its fury. The storm that confined itself to the course of the river. He was amazed that it never really reached Widenbridge. Only a couple of miles from the meteorological mayhem on the riverbank, the town, while washed in rain, missed the intensity of the blow.

After stowing his fishing equipment in his shed, Shrimp prepared the fish. With the sharpest of knives, he deftly removed the heads. Taking to the shoulder of the fish, he worked the knife along the backbone to the tail and expertly removed a clean fillet. Flipping the fish over, he took the other side of flesh from the skeleton. The second fish received the same treatment. As he worked, the ginger and white cat that belonged to a neighbour threaded herself, tail raised, between his calves.

"Righto Missie, here you go," said Shrimp as he flicked the innards of the catch to the feline. The next job was to skin the fillets. Before taking to the kitchen to cook his meal, Shrimp went across the back yard to see if the lemon tree had any ripe fruit. It was the only fruit bearing tree in the yard. It was a tree he nurtured with the most tender care.

MARGARET ATHERTON WAS BORN into a family that some would call upper middle class. Her father was a schools inspector. A man shaped by the military, he had been in the 'Big Show,' as he referred to the war. He was a loving husband and a strict, but understanding, father. To strangers, he had the air of authority. That authority, paired with genuine benevolence, made an ideal mix as he navigated his career path. It also endeared him to his children.

Mrs. Atherton loved and nurtured her children. Her twin sons, while intelligent, showed preference for rugged outdoor activities above academic pursuits. Still, both lads ranked highly at school. As a woman and a mother, she accepted the adage the boys will be boys. All three of her offspring showed some musical aptitude, but Margaret displayed more talent than her brothers. Like her siblings, Margaret was successful at school. She, too, had a sporting aptitude. Her fondness for the pool saw her constantly in the medals and ribbons at school and the swim club. If she had any physical aggression, it was given an avenue of release on the hockey field.

It was during her high school years, with the encouragement of her parents, that Margaret seriously undertook musical studies. Her preference was the piano. It was as if she and the instrument were created for each other. Not only had she the ability to play, she, remarkably, according to her tutor, had, for such a young person, the gift of composition. It was raw, but it was definitely within her.

WITH HIS STUDIES completed and exams passed with honours, Daniel Nolan was out of his khaki uniform and wearing a suit. He was now a detective. In order for him to find grounding as he entered this new phase of his career, he accepted a posting to Widenbridge.

The kettle on the gas stove boiled. As it whistled to alert that the tea was now ready to be brewed, Mrs. Rose Nolan smoothed down her skirt and reached for the caddy. Spooning leaf tea into her teapot, she smiled and said to her son. "This reminds me of you being six years old and playing cops and robbers with your cousins."

"Not quite Chicago of the 1920s and 30s," Dan told his mother.

"I pray not, Daniel, dear. I wish you were being sent somewhere closer, or they could find you a position here. Still, it is your career, son. I am truly proud of you and I know your father would have been, too. I don't think you'll be there long, anyway. You'll be too far away from your beloved fishing."

"Mum, I've checked it out. Widenbridge is sited on a river. According to the research I've done, the Wombadgalong River is a part of the system that before Federation and up to the outbreak of the First World War, was an integral part of paddle boat transportation. If there's a river, there'll be fish. Where there're fish, there'll be Daniel 'Shrimp' Nolan."

"You don't have to convince me of that, my boy," she replied while removing a tray of scones from the oven.

As FAR AS rural towns went, Widenbridge showed itself to be a prosperous community, boasting a state primary school, a Catholic primary school and a co-ed high school. There were five churches of different denominations. Three doctors, a dentist, a more than adequate hospital, four banks, two hotels, a Returned Services League, race club and various junior and senior sporting clubs flourished in the town. Being a centre for the surrounding farming community, Widenbridge had a couple of stock and station agents, three rural supply outlets, an agricultural machinery franchise, and a blacksmith.

The main street of the town, Kurrajong Street, was where the ladies of the town met for morning tea or lunch at the Coffee Cup Cafe. Parallel to the Wombadgalong River ran Loading Street, so named from the time barges were loaded with wool or grain. These would then meet up with the paddle steamers that once plied their trade along the eucalypt-lined arterial waterways that connected the major centres to the south.

A pretty town that showed civic pride. A cenotaph stood proudly in the town centre as a monument to the souls sacrificed on the battlefields abroad. The small but neat council chambers flew both the national and state standards. A colonial-style train station shyly showed itself from the edge of the town. The streets were wide, very wide, a legacy of the time when drays and bullock wagons ruled the carriageways.

RISING a couple of hundred miles to the east, the Wombadgalong River began its existence as a spring high in the ranges. The small, crystal stream found its natural course down the western slope of an insignificant mountain. The waters that would eventually join the great arterial waterways of the inland were added to by storm run-off and occasional snow-melt. Creeks that were often dry would gladly empty any water they carried into the growing Wombadgalong.

As far as rivers went, this waterway was neither a mighty river nor one that simply flowed on its way without major influence. A silvery aqua serpent it twisted and wriggled through the foothills until its spreading banks forced their path across the fertile plains.

Many were the peoples of the river. There were the ancients whose bones had long turned to dust. Still, their stories survived. Those young of the tribes, lost before history, who asked the wise elders how the river, the trees, the sky and stars came to be. They were the first to hear the legends.

Myths and imaginings of old men around a fire were born from the inquiring minds of those wanting to know.

Dozens of millennia later, hunters roamed the lightly wooded semi forests along the riverbanks. Women dug for edible roots or chased down small creatures that would add to a tribal meal. It was also the women who stripped bark from certain trees to work into a crude but effective twine which in turn made netting fish traps. The river people looked after their life source. The river, in return, looked after the people.

As time went on, the dynamics of the river and those who made her banks their home changed. New people with a new way of life dovetailed their way into the landscape. The old people, not knowing how to embrace change, kept to their ways. There was, of course, cross generational traffic that lived, or tried to live, by the old order and the new. Still, the river gave generously to those who required or desired her.

THE SUMMER SUN shone through the classroom windows. In the sun's rays, particles of dust hung in the air. The students were all chattering away excitedly. Earlier that day, the headmaster addressed the whole school assembly. His oration was to congratulate the senior students for completing their basic schooling and to wish them well with their endeavours and careers. No work was being done. Goodbyes were being said. Hugs and kisses were abundant when, at three o'clock that warm December afternoon, the school bell rang for the final time for Margaret Atherton and her year twelve class mates. It seemed an eternity since her mother held her hand and led her through the school gate on her first day of 'big school'. From kindergarten to the end of high school, it had been an amazing journey. Now a new path needed to be stepped upon. The path to adulthood and finding her place in society.

Discussions with her parents were insightful. There were many options. University, the public service, nursing, secretarial, journalism and other employments avenues discussed.

Margaret wasn't present at the conversation that would set her career in banking on track. It was a pleasant Sunday afternoon on the lawn bowls green that Percy Atherton and the man he was playing against were discussing children and their careers. Percy's singles opponent, David Bartlet, happened to be connected to the Royal Rural Banking Institution. It was suggested that there were many options in banking, not just being a teller. One could work towards investment, agricultural finance, international banking, stocks and shares and eventually branch management. Sure, being a teller was basic grounding, but the world of banking was wide and varied.

The following Wednesday, eighteen-year-old Margaret

was in an interview that would give her both a career and a change of life direction.

A few weeks later, Margaret received, by post, instructions to attend an introduction to the banking training course. It was there that five new potential bank employees were trained, tested, trained, and tested some more. Of the five, four were successful. From the four, Margaret led the pack. Another interview confirmed she had a banking career if she so desired. Initial placement would be in a city branch to give her a footing in the way things were done, as well as dealing with the public.

For the next three years, Margaret worked in various city branches before being posted to Widenbridge. Although she would be the junior staff member at Widenbridge, she knew the transfer to the country was her first big step up the ladder.

THERE WAS MORE than a hint of ice in the wind. The moon was so full it seemed that if anybody wanted to, they could pluck it from the sky. Not since he was a boy had the young detective experienced such a feeling of being alive.

The police station was, for the most part, fairly quiet. A few days after taking up his desk, Detective Daniel Nolan was designated his first case. It was then that he felt, if possible, even more alive.

Potentially, the case of a missing eight-year-old boy was as serious as a case could be. Was the child lost? Was he abducted, or worse? As expected, the boy's parents were in a state, especially the mother. Uniform police from Widenbridge and neighbouring Daneborough formed teams to scour the streets and surrounding bushland. Questions, endless questions, were being asked. The boy had to be somewhere.

Dan Nolan, while trained as a detective, was unprepared for such a case. How should he work it?

Shrimp Nolan, fisherman, knew how to work out a quarry. Applying angling skills and thought processes, Dan worked the case. Information was gleaned from the child's parents, teacher, siblings, and young friends. Questions were tossed about like burley. They were designed to attract the right snippet, the crucial lead. That lead came from a classmate.

It transpired that a handful of boys helped to liberate some lollies and a packet of cigarettes from a corner shop. Panic set in and the missing boy was told by his mates that, if they were caught, he'd go to gaol because he was the youngest in the group. The last time the recalcitrant lad was seen, he was heading back to the school yard. Dan knew this fish was frightened. He knew that a school yard crawling with coppers was not going to ease the situation.

Calling the uniform team away from the school, Dan, accompanied by a young policewoman, waited about twenty minutes. Night was falling. Trying to think as an eight-year-old was more difficult than he imagined. To catch a fish; think as a fish. Classrooms were shut for the day. The playground and equipment harboured only emptiness. Working around the outbuildings, Dan caught a slight scent of cigarette smoke. He pointed to the toilet block. How to do this? Whispering instructions to his offsider, Dan waited by the entrance. After being given the nod, the policewoman said loud enough for anyone to hear that the cleaning had been done for the day and the doors would be locked for the weekend.

The bait worked. Within seconds of the door closing, a sob came from inside. With care and compassion, laced with the right amount of authority, Detective Daniel Nolan of the

Widenbridge Police solved his first case. There was no follow-up court case. Trial, judgement, and punishment were in the hands of the various parents and the shopkeeper.

The case caused a stir, as such things did in small communities.

Working in a small country town bank was a long way removed from being a teller in the city. The basics were the same. People, mostly strangers, presented monetary deposits or requests for withdrawals, and that was that. The difference at the Widenbridge branch of the Royal Rural Banking Institution was the people. What would be a two-minute transaction in a city branch could extend to ten minutes or more with friendly chit-chat and could well finish up with an invitation to lunch or a barbecue on a Sunday afternoon.

It was during one such transaction being conducted by Detective Nolan that proved the genesis of his relationship with Margaret Atherton. It was not long before the two were more than bank teller and customer. Dan introduced Maggie to the world of country rugby. Maggie introduced Dan to the world of social niceties. Dan introduced Maggie, without much success, to the complexities of angling. Maggie introduced Dan, with an abundance of success, to homecooked dinners and loving female attention.

The two were made for each other.

Nothing raised curiosity in a country town like the wail of a siren. Add to that flashing light and a police escort clearing the way for a speeding ambulance. Cars pulled over to give clear passage. Respectable townsfolk instantly turned into gawkers. Gossips conjured up scenarios of what the problem could be. Policemen, ambos, doctors and nurses all knew they would be quizzed by most of whom they come into contact.

A small but dedicated medical team awaited the arrival of the ambulance just inside the floor to ceiling swinging doors that led to and from the emergency drive bay. The escorting police stood aside to permit the hospital team and the paramedics to ask and, in turn, answer questions of the patient.

With oxygen mask and fluid drip attached, the young woman, in her early to mid-twenties, was rushed into the emergency ward of the Widenbridge Base Hospital. She was found incoherent and barely conscious, slumped in a booth at the Coffee Cup Cafe.

Preliminary tests caused concern for the attending doctor. After stabilising his patient, he immediately called a city specialist about his concerns.

IN HIS KITCHEN, Shrimp prepared his meal. It was because he could cook that the meal, as basic as it appeared, was something splendid from such few ingredients. Two peeled but roughly cut potatoes substituted as chips, the fish, simply dipped in flour and put into a pan of sizzling oil. A thick slice of high-top bread spread thickly with butter rounded off the meal.

Reaching over, he took the freshly picked lemon from the windowsill and began rolling it over the corrugations of his kitchen sink. Slicing a wedge from the citrus fruit, he squeezed its juice over the fish to be finished for about eight minutes in a low-to-moderate oven.

Putting the remaining lemon on a saucer, he thought of the woman he loved. The woman he married and the woman who, even in death, still managed to give to him. He also remembered where he was, all those years ago, when he was radioed to attend Widenbridge Hospital post-haste.

WITH HIS SQUAD car's lights flashing blue and red and the siren warning other road users of an emergency, Detective Nolan swung the vehicle into the private car park at the hospital's rear. He raced into the out-patients section of the hospital. A senior nurse recognised Dan and stopped him by bracing his shoulders. She informed him that Maggie was undergoing tests and the doctor would be with him as soon as he was finished.

Dan Nolan was a mess. Every possible scenario, including some he'd never normally would have thought of, screened like a movie across his imagination. Fingernails dug deeply into his palms.

"Detective Nolan?"

Dan stood and without thought extended his hand and answered. "Yes, Dan Nolan."

While noticing Dan's firm handshake, Dr. Bryan Edmonds asked his patient's husband to accompany him into an interview room. "Dan, I may call you Dan, yes? Dan, I believe your wife may have some kind of issue with her brain. By the information I have gleaned, she groaned, clasped at both her temples and passed out. The initial tests indicate, and our investigation is preliminary, that the problem is cerebral, not heart, lung, kidney or a reproductive pathology."

"She'll be alright though Doctor, won't she? She can come home, if not now, tomorrow?"

"Dan, we cannot do the tests required here. We'll have to send her to the city. My feeling is, and I'll pray for her sake and yours that I'm wrong, that this could be something very serious. Nothing will be known until proper tests can be carried out. With your permission, I'd like to arrange for immediate transfer to the city where specialist testing and treatment can be set in place."

As a distant intercom sounded muffled in the background and hospital staff went about their daily duties, Dan turned pale under the fluorescent lighting. He saw nothing. All he felt was numb. "She will be alright, won't she?" he asked. "She will be alright!" this time making it sound as a command. "Sorry, Dr Edmond, sorry, yes, yes, do anything that will make her better."

The doctor reached over and taking hold of Dan's wrists, looked the policeman, the husband of his charge, in the eyes and said as gently as he could, "Dan this may be very serious, do you understand? I'm telling you Margaret may be in a struggle for her life. If that is the case, she won't get better. Prepare yourself for that outcome, Dan. I can't tell you how to do that, but I'm here to help you and Margaret any way I can."

Looking straight back at the medical man, Daniel Nolan wept.

THE DAY still held a promise of rain. Shrimp had finished his meal and completed the post-lunch clean up. A strong breeze rattled the windows on the northern side of the house. He didn't like days like this. He couldn't go fishing or work in the yard. He hated being housebound.

Out of want for something to do, he found a tin of

furniture polish and set to work putting a shine on the piano. Apart from some photographs and a reel of home-movie film, the piano was the only thing in the house that was Maggie's. The refurbished 1930s 'Thos. Goggan and Bros.' piano was his wedding gift to his bride. How he loved to hear and see her play; how she loved to play.

He recalled a time when Maggie, though ill, would sit and play. She would play songs of her childhood, songs that were popular of the day, or songs she composed herself.

Sitting on the stool, Dan absent-mindedly polished the lid protecting the keyboard.

His mind went back to an afternoon, some decades before. He had finished work just a little early. Walking along the path in their front yard, past the rose bed, the hedge of sacred bamboo, the geraniums and other flowers of which he never knew the name, he heard a soft, sweet melody. The piece was unfamiliar to him. It had the touch of a lullaby about it. Quietly, he let himself into the house and waited for Maggie to finish playing. "That was beautiful, Darl, what was it?"

"Dan! I never heard you come home. It was just a little something I put together. It was something to match my mood. Sorry, Dan, I was feeling a little melancholy, and this just seemed to ease the situation."

"A pretty tune, do you have any words?"

"Well yes, but they are the words of a girl feeling a little sorry for herself."

"A bad day?"

"Oh Dan! I'm happy within myself. We both accept the situation, but sometimes 'Mr. Bad Thoughts' creeps into my head. This song, while maybe seen as being a little self-pitying, helped chase the bad man in my head away."

"Would you sing it for me? If Mr. Bad Thoughts shows up

again, I'll handcuff him and take him down to the cells and forget I put him there."

Maggie smiled, squeezed Dan's hand, then played the chords of the introduction.

She sang,

> *"Let me sleep, little Darling, sleep.*
> *"Let me sleep, little Darling, sleep.*
> *"I'm tired. Let me rest, my head on your breast.*
> *"Let me sleep, little Darling, sleep.*
>
> *"Let me sleep, little Darling, sleep.*
> *"Let me sleep, little Darling, sleep.*
> *"The day has been long, I'm burdened by wrong.*
> *"Let me sleep, little Darling, sleep.*
>
> *"Let me sleep, little Darling, sleep.*
> *"Let me sleep, little Darling, sleep.*
> *"The mountains I climb aren't all in my mind.*
> *"Let me sleep, little Darling, sleep.*
>
> *"Let me sleep little Darling, sleep.*
> *"Let me sleep little Darling, sleep.*
> *"There's no moon tonight, I'll be alright,*
> *"If you, let me sleep, little Darling, sleep.*
>
> *"Let me sleep little Darling, sleep.*
> *"Let me sleep, little Darling, sleep.*
> *"I'm tired. Let me rest, in your sweet softness.*
> *"Let me sleep, little Darling, sleep.*
>
> *"Let me sleep, little Darling, sleep.*
> *"Let me sleep, little Darling, sleep."*

Not for the first time, they embraced and cried. The tears were not tears of sadness or pity; they were tears of love.

Dan put the polish away.

THE CANCER that made its home in Maggie's brain was more than aggressive. It was cruel and violent. It wasted no time in robbing a vibrant woman of her prime. Thoughts of conceiving and raising a family were the first to be extinguished. As she lost weight and her health, she maintained her spark of life. Her love for her husband and friends grew. Above all, she retained, if not increased, both her faith and her sense of humour.

BEREFT OF TEARS, Dan sat in his living room with his mother and his in-laws. Conversation was awkward. Dan was a practical man. He knew that with Maggie's passing, he would have to get on with things as best he could. Not for Maggie's sake, nothing would bring her back, but because that was what had to be done.

The knock on the door presented those gathered with an excuse to have their thoughts distracted. Mrs. Nolan made to go to the door, but Dan said he'd go. Muffled voices from the front doorway could be heard. Mrs. Atherton asked if anybody would like some tea. Out of wont for something to say, those in the room all said, "yes."

"Well, smack me down and paint me green," Dan said as he entered the room carrying a large woven cane basket almost overflowing with food. "That was Sadie Rhodes, she dropped by some cooking. So nice of her. Amazing, really amazing."

"It isn't uncommon, Daniel, for friends and neighbours to give gifts of food in these circumstances," said Shrimp's mother. "Anyway, dear, who is Sadie Rhodes?"

"Mum, she is the wife of one of the local small-time crims. A few years ago, I helped put her husband, Jock, away for three months for helping himself to some of the church's Communion wine. At the time, he and a few mates were having a bit of a party and the drinks were running low. Jock was always one for a scheme and he reckoned a few bottles from the Sunday House would be as good as anything else, even better if he didn't have to exchange some legal tender for it."

Mrs. Atherton returned with a tray holding a teapot, cups, saucers, milk and sugar. Everybody thanked her. "Sorry to have interrupted, Daniel. What were you saying?"

Dan reiterated and continued. "Seems that while Jock was on his leave of incarceration, Maggs, without my knowledge, was keeping an eye on Sadie and their three little kiddies. Sadie was telling me that every Thursday, when Jock was in gaol, Maggie would take around a basket of food and some sweets for the Rhodes family. Just so they would have one decent meal a week. Sadie said that once in a while, there would be a toy for each of the children. She said that Maggie told her it was just between Sadie and herself and not to tell anybody, especially me, it seems. I invited her in, but she declined saying this," pointing to the hamper, "was the least the Rhodes family could do."

SCHOOL CHILDREN MARCHED in parallel lines towards their classroom. The morning was bright. The bushes and treetops danced a wispy waltz to the tune of a breeze with just a hint of coolness. The church adjacent to the school began to fill with mourners.

Hands were shaken, cheeks were kissed, and condolences extended. Members of the constabulary arrived in full uniform to support their brother-in-mourning.

As the final note of the opening hymn faded, the minister addressed the grieving. He spoke words from the Holy Bible. He related that Jesus, in His humanness, grieved when told that Lazarus had died. "'Jesus wept,' it says in the Gospel of John, and as the situation dictates, so should you. Elsewhere, King Solomon, the Wise, wrote in Ecclesiastes, that God sets a time for birth and the time for death, a time for sorrow—a time for joy, a time for mourning and a time for dancing. Cry now, but let the love of our sister Margaret bring dancing to your hearts, which she will do when the time is right."

Outside, a dove cooed as she alighted on the frame of an open window. Inside, the mid-morning sun illuminated the aisle and the pulpit.

When given introduction by the minister, Maree Hillard, Maggie's long-time friend, made her way to the microphone. She swiped away a tear with the index finger of her left hand, sniffed, and took a deep breath. Thoughtfully, the minister passed her a small pack of tissues. She nodded her thanks.

"Dan, Mr. and Mrs. Atherton, family, friends and strangers, this isn't, I'm sure, how we'd plan to spend a beautiful morning. It is a morning such as this that Margaret would find beauty. Margaret, uh! Um, she really didn't like Margaret. Maggie found beauty in just about everything. She found it easier to give love rather than express dislike. I don't think she knew how to hate. Maggie,

Margaret Therese Nolan, was a daughter, a sister, and a wife. She was a friend. She was a musician, a composer, a writer, and a great teller of jokes. She was a bank teller and, if you know her history, a bank robber. Wow! Wasn't that an episode in her life? She never robbed the bank, of course, but was almost framed for doing so. She often joked that life would have been champagne and caviar had she done so.

"Maggie worked selflessly for various charities. She volunteered at the rugby club, she assisted at the preschool centre. Every year she was involved in the Carols by Candlelight in the town square. Never did she ask for payment or return the favour. All she did, in a practical way, was show love. She gave generously, never wanting or expecting to be given to in return. How embarrassed would she be if she could see the love that has gathered here this morning?

"It was about eleven days ago she called me. Sick as she was, her thoughts were for each and every one of you. It was her idea to hold a 9 o'clock funeral service because she didn't want you waking up and waiting hours to 'get it over and done with'. It was Maggie who organised the wake at the Brigalow Hotel with instructions for Mrs. Atherton to get 'Old Perc' to let his hair down, and for 'Perc not to get my Danny too drunk.'" An uncomfortable giggle permeated the congregation.

"Maggie also chose the hymns and the Bible verses and she said if she could have a final wish, it would be that no tears be shed. As if, Maggs!"

A chuckle, unrestricted, rippled through the church.

"Her desire is to be cremated without fuss. The only stipulation, which I understand she settled with Dan, is that he holds her ashes at home. When the time comes, he will be told what to do. He's a detective, and he is a fisherman; he knows how to be patient.

"Before I left her on that last visit those few days ago, she reached under her pillow and handed me an envelope. 'Please read this as my final message to everyone?' she asked." Reaching for a tissue, Maree wiped her eyes, smiled, and read:

"One day I will not write anymore, I will not laugh, I will not cry or know anymore. One day when I when I am just a memory, remember me with love and smiles. Remember, I never meant to hurt you. I only wanted to love you in at least one of the images of love. Remember never any tears, but always the joy. Please, don't wish for what was, or will be; be pleased for what was. I trust you'll wipe away any pain, from whatever source, with a recollection of a time we shared. A time now gone, but not taken from us. A time we both, unknowingly, let slip by.

"When you laugh, don't let anything I've done dampen your good cheer and mirth. If that is the case, I'd rather you forget me. I hope you don't. I cannot express in words what is felt in the heart. Some can. I never could. Sometimes, inside, I feel part of me has been stolen. The part of me to love for the sake of love. It was stolen when I didn't know what was being taken and, too late, I tried to live without it. I must live without it until it is replaced.

"Although we were a long time ago, I often feel you and talk to you. I laugh or frown at the things you would do or say. I've never been alone, only lonely. Even sometimes when we were together, I was lonely. One day I won't be lonely or alone, but I'll still remember you with a smile; and when you are in the cold and dark, I'll be reaching out to you to show you the way without stumbling.

"One day when I sing my song, you will be in the chorus,

but as yet the music is not written and the words do not rhyme. One day my dance will be finished and so will yours. Who will care? The rivers will always flow, the birds will always fly, but one day I will not write anymore. I will not laugh; I will not cry or know anymore. One day, when I am just a memory, remember me with love and smiles."

Maree sniffed more tears away and finished with, "That, dear friends, is the heart and soul of Margaret Therese Nolan. Love you Maggs, miss you, mate." In an unabashed flood of tears, Maree returned to her pew.

THE INCLEMENT WEATHER of the day before had cleared. The new day was watched over by a sky, the electric blue of which could only be found in an opal. Unlike the previous day, this day gave Shrimp the opportunity to get into some yard work.

Pruning he found therapeutic. The hedge had a trim. The two rose bushes were cut back almost to ground level. He recalled Maggie saying years ago, prune roses hard, they love it. Where the deciduous trees had dropped leaves, Shrimp pruned the bare twigs just for good measure.

With the pruning done it was time to mow. These days he never considered mowing a chore. He recalled his late father almost having to force his son into mowing the yard. The machine of Dan's young years was an old two stroke. The spark plug was forever clogging with carbon and needed cleaning by dipping it in some fuel and scrubbing it with a wire brush. The next stage was to thread a rope around the head of the fly and pull hard enough to create compression to fire the spark plug thus starting the engine. Thinking back on it, it was probably that mower that had a young Daniel Nolan using what his mother called 'shed words'.

The grass cutter he used these days had an electric start, mulching capabilities and a catcher. Luxury!

THREE MONTHS after Maggie's funeral it was Shrimp's birthday. It was not a day he was looking forward to. All the birthdays he had while he and Maggie were together, he always received something to do with fishing. She always knew what he needed.

Life was returning to normal. It was a new and different kind of normal, but one he knew he had to adapt to. Work at Widenbridge Police Station, involvement with the Quolls Rugby Club and fishing kept him occupied although not thoroughly distracted from the absence of his wife.

While he was fiddling with a new knot he'd read about in an angling magazine a voice called to him from the side of the house. "Whozit? I'm around the back." Looking up, he witnessed a bush in a pot being carried down the pathway. Patty Hume, the Widenbridge Nursery owner popped her head from behind the greenery.

"Detective Nolan? Good, I have a little birthday present for you."

"Oh!" said Dan. "Who from?"

"Can't tell you, but you'll be surprised."

"Thanks, Patty, what do I owe you for delivery?

"Nothing, all taken care of. There's a card attached, catch you later, bye."

When he saw the card his heart almost stopped. The handwriting was Maggie's. Opening the envelope he removed the card and read, 'My Darling Daniel, happy birthday. Sorry I can't be with you in person, but if you follow my instructions I'll be with you forever. This lemon tree is to be planted in full sunlight, towards the back, in the middle of our backyard. Dig a hole twice deep enough to cover the roots and about twice as wide. Now, take my ashes and mix them with the soil to fill in the hole when you've planted the tree. I'll help the tree to grow and keep you in all the lemons you'll ever need to juice onto any fish you catch and cook. I miss you, you kind sweet man, but I'll always be a part of your existence, as you are with mine. Eternal love, Maggie.'

Surprising himself with his reaction Shrimp laughed and laughed until he cried. His Maggie had found a way to be with him, and for him to be with her. Only Maggie could find ways to continue to give love, even after passing. That lemon tree never stopped producing fruit, and it never lacked any attention from Shrimp.

THE END

A BLAST FROM THE PAST

Frightened by the intensity of the scream, a scream conceived in pain then born in pure agony, birds took to the wing. About eighteen feet up the twisted trunk of an ancient eucalyptus tree, a possum, with her young clinging to her back, was returning to her hollow in the big tree and stopped her climb. Her huge eyes, designed to see in the dark, ignored the surrounding vista of the river with a gossamer sheet of late autumnal fog floating like a spectre above the water, the distant rolling hills and the people below, to stare at the source of the disturbance. She blinked, a slow blink of nonchalance, and silently entered her home.

On the ground, in a small clearing with gunyahs built around a central fire, the naked man was delirious with pain. The aboriginal woman, on whose lap he rested, bathed his feverish head and made soothing, nurturing sounds. Wide-eyed children stood staring at the near-dead white stranger the men had brought into their midst.

The burns the man was suffering were horrific. The hunters belonging to the tribe had found him collapsed in a shallow creek and carefully carried him back to camp. The woman was given charge of the man. Diligently, she applied a poultice of crushed witchetty grubs and sugarbag, the pure sweet honey produced by the tiny, stingless native bees. Thousands of years of bush medicine lore worked through her gentle hands. Drawing on an aeon of knowledge sung by generation after generation, she knew that the crushed grubs had a soothing effect and helped heal the skin. The honey's antibacterial properties helped to fight infection.

The scream left the man exhausted. He collapsed into a personal oblivion.

SUNDAY MORNINGS COULD BE quiet at the best of times. This particular Sunday morning seemed more so. Not too far off in the distance, perched on a fence rail, a kookaburra laughed at the lone figure seated on the platform of the Widenbridge railway station. A recalcitrant scrap of paper, an ice-cream wrapper, no doubt discarded by one of the town's children, tumbled gently along the platform propelled by just a ghost of a breeze. Rising from his seat, Dan Nolan, without thought, looked about the deserted station and beyond, before deftly scooping the litter from the ground to place in the bin outside the Station Master's office. Again, the jackass laughed.

"Cheeky bugger," Dan said to himself.

From the far end of Kurrajong Street, a church bell pealed. Its metallic notes spread as if a musical flood across the quiet town. Memories stirred in his mind. Memories of Sunday mornings when he was a boy. For no particular reason, his father's voice permeated his thoughts. Smiling, Dan recalled the words he just imagined his late father saying.

"No matter where it is on this Earth, son, there is nothing as lonely as an empty train station."

"True, Dad, very true," Dan muttered in a half whisper.

Dan Nolan had, some years before, retired from the police force. He had made Widenbridge his home and saw no reason to leave the quaint inland town which had taken him to heart and vice-versa. Normally, on a Sunday morning, if anybody bothered to look, they'd find him somewhere on the bank of the Wombadgalong River trying to entice a member of the piscatorial population to invite itself to Dan's to be lunch. Dan, or Shrimp as most folk knew him, had always been a keen angler. He had entertained the thought of wetting a line this particular morning, but resisted the temptation due to the fact he was to meet the train.

The sound of a key opening a lock caught his attention. Turning, he saw the assistant station-master, Claude Ellis.

"G'day Mr Nolan. Waitin' on the train, eh?"

"Yeh! You'd make a top detective, Claude. Just want to pick up a parcel."

"Well, you might be waiting for a while. I just received a telegraph saying the rails on the other side of Daneborough buckled in the heat a couple of days back. Gangers have just about got the job done, but the train won't be in for about three quarters of an hour, maybe a bit more. You waiting on some new fishin' stuff?"

"Something like that. Right, Claude, thanks for letting me know. I'm in no hurry."

"Good-o then Mr Nolan, I'll leave ya to it," said Claude and returned to the office.

With time to kill, Dan crossed the tracks to wander along the street when for no reason he entered the Widenbridge cemetery. Like cemeteries everywhere, the Widenbridge graveyard was a local history book, if one cared to look.

Strolling along the rows, Dan took in the names of those who made their mark on this now quiet, but not unimportant, country town. There were those who were laid to rest in the latter part of the 1800s. Names that belonged to many of the families which still make up the population of Widenbridge. There were the graves of babies whose parents didn't have the medical assistance of this day. Dan felt an odd, but calming, sadness as he read of more than one young woman who died in childbirth. At the far end of the cemetery was the Dedicated War Garden. No bodies lay below the headstones, each of which featured a carved poppy and the names and rank of those who fell on distant battle fields. Those names were also engraved on the cenotaph that stood proudly in Kurrajong Street.

"Lest we forget," Dan whispered.

Many of the marble or granite headstones had worn over the years. Some legends were almost impossible to decipher.

As it was with cemeteries, especially in country towns, this one was segregated into religious denominations. There were sections for Presbyterian, Church of England, Roman Catholic, Methodist, and others. Much of the area was secular.

Reaching the end of the row, Dan turned to make his way back to the station when one neglected headstone captured his eye. What was remarkable was the fact that the information supplied displayed as much ignorance about the interred as it did knowledge. It read 'Below, the ground holds to her bosom the mortal remains of Kelly Daniels. Date of Birth - Unknown. Age - Unknown. Died twelfth day of October 1937.'

What stirred Dan's detective interest was the fact that he didn't know of any family by the name of Daniels in Widenbridge or any of the surrounding towns.

THE INFERNO MELTED the glass in the already cracked and broken windows. The wooden structure permeated by countless applications of protective greases and oils aided the flames rather than deterred them. Slabs, hewn from local bush timber, that formed the roof outside and the ceiling inside, held years' worth of dried gum leaves and twigs. Once the tongues of flame tasted the moistureless vegetation, their appetite increased for more of the combustible fuel.

At the time of the fire, the surrounding area was encased in an aura of bright orange from the flames and black from the smoke. Before the blaze really took hold, small animals that sheltered under the floorboards scurried into the nearby bush for safety. Rats that made their nests in the wall cavities soon found escape through holes in the structure. Snakes, unseen by those above, slithered hurriedly from the growing heat.

Outside, there were those who did all they could to promote the conflagration. They were congregated by the front, their attention focused on the results of their actions. Had one or more of those thought of going to the back of the building, they may have witnessed one man making his way into the nearby bush discarding his burning clothing as he painfully stumbled from tree to tree, escaping the fire and those feeding it.

SOME DAYS later Shrimp was casting his new lures, with his new rod and reel, into the waters of the Wombadgalong River, flowing so slowly it could have been molasses. He'd been there since the dawn. He had watched the stars slowly fade as the new day, heralded by an orchestra of bird-song, announced its arrival. The fish were on the bite early on but had in the past half hour or so gone quiet.

"Time to have a brew," Shrimp mused as walked the riverbank to collect enough firewood to boil his billy.

A gentle south-westerly breeze had the higher leaves of the trees performing an arboreal cotillion. A flash of dark-tan fur teased the Shrimp's eye for a dash of a second. Unconsciously and fleetingly, he thought: water-rat or maybe a platypus. Tea made, Shrimp sat nibbling at a slab of rich fruit cake and sipped his cup. He was lost in his thoughts.

"Penny for 'em Dan?"

Startled, Shrimp turned, smiled and said, "Crikey, Milt, you just took a decade off me years. What ya upta?"

For many years, Milt de Grey was the chief journalist with the Widenbridge Word newspaper, locally known simply as the 'Word'. Like Shrimp, he was now retired.

"I was just going nowhere for no reason when I spied your ute and thought I'd see how they were biting. Hadn't seen you around for a while, but that's not unusual."

"Grab a mug, mate, and help yourself to the billy. Sorry, I just knocked off the cake, but if you want a dash of rum in your tea, you're more than welcome. You'll find it in my tackle bag."

"Thanks, I could go a cuppa. You seemed somewhat lost in thought."

"You know of a family, or more likely a bloke by the surname of Daniels? When I was waiting for last Sunday's train to bring in this new fishing gear, I went for a bit of a wander through the bone-yard. Interesting places are cemeteries. Anyhow, I stumbled across this plot from the thirties, thirty-seven I recall, bloke by the name of Kelly Daniels. You know, Milt, I don't know of anyone around here with the back-name Daniels. They don't know when or where he was born and no idea how old he was. Bit of a mystery. It's whetted the soul of this old detective, I'll tell you."

"Can't say I know the name, mate. Tell you what, name a day, shout me beer and I'll take you into the archives of the Word and we'll do a bit of grave digging through the pages of the Widenbridge past."

"Righto Milt. You're on."

It took more than his strength to flee the fire. The pain of his burns confused him and he wandered aimlessly through the scrub. The survival instinct, not just to live, but to keep moving away from the fire and the cheering of the animated congregation drove his legs as if they had a mind of their own. He had no idea where he was going. Ripping the shirt from his body and stepping from his charred moleskins, he staggered through the lightly timbered bushland. Something inside his head warned him not to scream. Its message was that 'screaming was danger'.

Rafts of skin tore agonisingly from his arms and chest as he, drunken-like, slammed into trees. Due to the pain, his nose, itself blistered and swollen from the flames, could not register the scent of his singed beard and hair.

There was another burning in his left shoulder. It was different from the fire burns.

The afternoon soon gave way to nightfall. In the fading light and by pure good luck, he found a slow-flowing creek. In a fog of agony that blurred all his senses, he lowered himself into the cool, relief-offering water. Fortuitously, a log lay parallel to the creek bank. It substituted as a pillow to keep his head above the creek surface.

The pain eased, but the confusion intensified. Head

resting on the log, his skyward-looking eyes did not, could not, focus on the stars scattered across the firmament. Still refusing to acknowledge the tortuous pain caused by the fire, he gave way to unconsciousness.

The hunting party found him the next morning.

WISPS OF CONDENSED steam rose from their tea mugs as the retired detective and journalist searched through files of microfiche. Starting in 1937, and working backwards, the two set about attempting to find the jigsaw pieces that hopefully would mould together some kind of history relating to Kelly Daniels. Adjusting his reading glasses, Shrimp said that they may have to go back decades to discover their quarry.

MONTHS PASSED. The white man with the burns was recovering well. His gentle nurse had brought him from near certain death to being able to travel, albeit stiffly, with the tribe. He was still in no condition to hunt with the men, but, due to the fact that he was no stranger to living in and from the bush, was content to assist the women with camp duties and gathering from the bush for seasonal foods.

His memories, before the fire, were as clear as a crisp winter's sky. He could not recall how or where the hunters found him. Still, he was glad they did. The tribal elders were abundant in their generosity when it came to having their people attend to the suffering stranger.

"TELL YOU WHAT, Milt, there's some interesting reading here."

"Too right, the entire history of the district. Almost. Not much on your old mate, Kelly Daniels."

"Something will turn up, surely," replied Shrimp. "I did come across a name that rang a bell, though. A bloke called Ewan Rickard, you know of him?"

"No, no... no, I don't think... yes I do, Rickard, bit of a derro-looking fellow, liked to gamble a bit, that him?"

"You've nailed him. So did I, not long after I lobbed into Widenbridge. An eccentric. He was pretty old then, but still! It was Maggie put me onto him. She was pretty new to town as well, had a job, as you probably know, at the Royal Rural Banking Institution, and we'd just started knockin' around together. Anyway, she tells me about this old fella, backside outta his trousers, not seen a razor for almost a week and wearing odd shoes. Not strange shoes, odd shoes, like odd socks. One lace-up the other was fastened by a buckle. He rocks up to the counter this day. Well old, stuck-up Mrs Riggs turned her nose towards the ceiling and directed Rickard to Maggie's teller booth. Maggs reckoned Riggsie almost fell out of her flannel knickers when the old bloke throws over a paper bag with about three thousand, maybe a bit more, in it."

Milt's eyes opened wide. His eyebrows were raised so high they almost met his hairline. "Really! Where did he get that from?"

"C'mon, let's go across to the Brig for lunch and I'll tell you about it."

AS TIME WENT BY, the pain of the burns subsided. The scarring was atrocious. The middle and ring fingers of his left hand were fused together. The once handsome face that proudly wore a barbered moustache was stretched and strained, so much so that his right eye was almost at the point of being permanently closed. About a third of his scalp was devoid of hair. His legs weren't badly affected, but his upper torso and neck highlighted the seriousness of the man's injuries. He bore no resemblance to his pre-fire self, so much so that he even appeared shorter. Such was the extent of the scarring. His wounded left shoulder was not as strong as it once was.

Physically, he was a different man.

The nurturing from the woman had saved the man's life.

He soon picked up enough of the tribal tongue, mainly from the young children who themselves were learning their native language, to be able to communicate with his saviours.

Although he was now fit enough to hunt with the men, he was unable to do so due to the fact he was not an initiated member of the tribe. His duties were confined to working with the women, although that too was restricted by the rituals that were for women only.

He was accepted, but he wasn't part of their world. Still, he was extremely grateful for what these people had done for him and he saw it as his duty to contribute and do anything to assist the tribe in their daily routine.

Of an evening, he would occasionally entertain his bemused hosts with lilting or sometimes rousing songs from his mother's homeland.

He often held conversations with himself in English and would write letters to home in the dust.

IN THE BEER garden of the Brigalow Hotel, the two men sipped their beer and waited for their mixed grill lunches to arrive. The atmosphere was relaxing. In the background, a radio, perched on a shelf behind the bar, broadcast the mid-week races. A grapevine grew and twisted its way through and over the trellised barricade that separated the beer garden from the street to the rear. The air was barely disturbed by the blades of a large pedestal fan which turned all but pointlessly. Across Loading Street, the Wombadgalong River could be glimpsed, making its forever wandering to the west.

As a willy-willy danced across a dusty flat, memories also waltzed through Shrimp's mind.

Suddenly, Milt de Grey started with a soft giggle that erupted into a full-blown laugh. "What's so funny?" asked Shrimp as he took a long pull at his beer.

"I was just wondering," replied Milt still giggling, "how the hell did you know old Myrtle Riggs wore flannel knickers?"

Shrimp immediately saw the humour in his friend's question. He tried, in vain, to suppress his own laughter. Half the beer in his mouth found liberty, via his nostrils, in a fine mist spray which Shrimp tried to direct to the floor of the beer garden.

HE COULD NOT TELL how long he had been wandering with the tribe. He knew it was years. Many landmarks became familiar, and he himself became more than familiar with many ways to survive in the bush.

As time went by, the landscape changed. Settlers took up selections, grew crops, ran cattle and sheep as they played their part in opening up a land that, to its nomadic peoples, was already open.

The elders decided that they needed to rearrange their

area and movement. The white man, as much a part of the tribe as many others, had no part in their future.

It was a parting he knew was coming. So, after two decades, they parted ways at the extreme northern border of the tribal territory. One last time, he thanked those who saved him from eternal darkness and brought him to where he now was. The woman who nursed him so long ago had been married into a different, but related, tribe.

Keeping to the river, as best he could, he knew he'd have no problem with collecting food.

***

GAMBLING HAD ALWAYS BEEN a passion of men in the bush. It was one of the few entertainments they had. Horse racing spawned a type of gambler that was looking for a quick tally.

Ewan Rickard was a gambler; it was in his blood. He ran a two-up school, illegal gatherings in the form of rough casinos, fights, football, dogs and, of course, the horses.

Shrimp explained to Milt it was an elaborate scheme with the horses that was the downfall of Rickard.

It was too many years ago, but the memory was as fresh as this morning's breakfast.

In those days, as it was now, Saturday was race day right across the country. No matter where you were, you could listen to the nags on the local radio. Little stations were the conduit between the various racecourses and the punter. The pub on a Saturday arvo was the centre of the racing universe. Drinkers, punters, S.P. bookies, ladies, dressed in finery and sipping shandies in the beer-garden would get their husbands to place a small wager here and there on their behalf.

On this particular Saturday, the local radio was covering the races from the major centres and also the once-a-year country meeting from Mt Brookline about one hundred and sixty miles away, but close enough to hold a strong local interest.

Ewan Rickard had wormed his way into the good books of Trev Ryan, the sports announcer at the radio station at Danebrough. Like most, Ryan enjoyed a bet, but working while the races were on made it difficult. Rickard said he had a plan that would make them both some money and they only had to be a little smart about it.

Back then, the radio was the only link to the local racecourses. The major city races came via relay through the radio network. With local races the announcer would listen on a separate line, direct from the track, and would broadcast the races as they were called, or if they clashed with a major-centre race, the announcer would record the country race on a tape and replay it immediately after the city event. What Rickard devised, drawing on the knowledge of Trev Ryan, was close to flawless.

Milt was keen to know more.

* * *

THE MID-MORNING SUN WAS GENTLE. He was pleased that it was. The hot sun of summer aggravated the more major scars he bore.

Cresting a hill, he saw an emu with half a dozen striped chicks trotting behind. Not too long ago, this would have been cause for a quick hunt and a sensational feast. The tribesmen would have provided the music with clap-sticks and boomerangs. All members would partake in the corroboree that would have lasted hours. Members of his tribe, and he felt he belonged to the tribe, would re-enact the success of the day.

Catching emus was relatively easy. The big, flightless bird has an insatiable curiosity. The act of providing something out of the ordinary, something like waving a woven basket overhead on the end of a spear would soon have the bird's attention. As it came to investigate, hunters hidden and dead still in the surrounding grasses, would pick their moment then pounce on their quarry.

That was not to be the case this day. Down in the valley floor was a small, neat homestead, not much larger than a hut. Keeping himself sheltered in the trees, he sat and waited. No smoke rose from the lean-to kitchen at the back. He looked for evidence of dogs. Nothing.

The sun climbed high and shadows changed direction.

With a caution bred into him from both his earlier, younger, almost forgotten life and the time spent with the tribe, he approached the building.

Wearing a basic woven grass skirt and a belt made from plaited human hair around his waist to hold a couple of tools doubling as weapons. Any witness to him would swear they were seeing a real white black-fella. They would have been shocked by the scarring on his body, not to mention his distorted and guttural speech.

Nobody saw him.

"Now, the thing is," Shrimp was telling Milt, "timing. Timing is everything. You see, in order to make his financial killing, Rickard needed Ryan's technical know-how and broadcaster's sense of timing. The trick was to use time to fool the listeners, bookmakers included, into thinking things had changed, just a little. Rickard knew the Mt. Brookline races were broadcast direct from the course by a P.M.G.

landline, via the telephone exchange, to the studio. It was a one-way line, so really the people at the racecourse couldn't listen back to the broadcast. In fact, they had no idea if their race calls were being broadcast or not. That's the genius of the plan."

Milt looked baffled. "I don't understand," he said. "What's so ingenious about that?"

"Well," said Shrimp, "what Ryan had to do was make a regular announcement that due to some 'unforeseen incident' at the track, all races had been put back by ten minutes. Then he'd record the Mt. Brookline races, as they were called, and replay each race ten minutes or so after they had been run.

The downfall was announcing that the course ambulance had been delayed en route to the racetrack, hence the delay.

"So, what happened, Dan? How did it fall apart?"

"Fate, stepped in, I suppose. I was having lunch one day at the Coffee Cup Café when Bede O'Hara, the bookmaker, spied me and asked if he could bend my ear. He told me that he was having a beer with Paul Hill, the ambulance driver, and happened to ask him if he was on duty at the Mt. Brookline races. Paul said he was and asked why. Bede inquired as to what caused the ambulance to be delayed and Paul told him it wasn't. The ambulance was at the track half an hour before the first race. Bede informed Hill that, according to the bloke on the wireless, the races were all delayed by ten minutes. Paul Hill said that wasn't the case. It was one of those few events he'd attended that ran like clockwork.

"Well, old Bede turned to me and asked if I knew Rickard. I said I'd heard of him, due to the incident at the bank, but didn't know him. Then Bede proceeded to tell me that Rickard almost cleaned him out by having an unprecedented run of luck at the Mt. Brookline meeting. Two of the winners were absolute long-shots that not even their owners would have backed and Rickard just kept on winning.

"Do you see what was happening, Milt?"

"I think so. Ryan recorded the races, replayed them ten minutes late, consistently as to not draw any undue attention, passed the winners and place-getters onto Rickard, by telephone, who was placing his bets with O'Hara. Right?"

"Spot on," Shrimp smiled, "He gave Ryan a cut, a smallish cut I would imagine, and banked the rest. That's where fate stepped in. Maggie told me about the amusing incident at the bank. Paul Hill crossed paths with Bede O'Hara and Rickard wasn't smart enough to place his bets with three or four other bookies.

"After talking to Bede, we started an investigation. I took a trip out to Mt. Brookline, talked to the jockey club officials and confirmed that all ran to schedule. I took statements from both Paul Hill and Bede O'Hara before heading to Daneborough to have a conversation with the manager of the radio station. Before he called in Trevor Ryan, he took me into a technical room with lots of recorders and things. He located a tape of the day of the race meeting, found the place where the races would have been, and we both heard Ryan's announcements of the delayed races. The manager laughed and said Ryan could have saved being charged by the police and dismissed from the radio station had he been at least half smart and wiped the tape that recorded everything that goes to air. A logger tape they call it. All radio stations have them. It's a legal requirement, and it acts as a safeguard for the station."

"Pretty elaborate," said Milt.

"Too elaborate for their own good. Too greedy and not smart enough. So, my friend, there you have my dealings with Ewan Rickard. I'd forgotten about him until today. An early victory in the book of Detective Daniel Nolan, Widenbridge Police," Shrimp said smilingly and raising his glass in mock salute.

IF HE LEARNED anything from his years with the tribe, it was how to track and how not to be tracked. He was, should there have been anyone looking where he was, as close to perfectly camouflaged as possible. High mares'-tail clouds drifted lethargically in the high afternoon blue sky. He listened. Magpies swooped acrobatically as they chased insects around the building. A snap of a dead twig exploded like a bomb in his ears. He froze. Turning almost imperceptibly, he managed a twisted smile as a wombat waddled from its hole to start a forage for food or maybe a mate.

The breeze was blowing into him, which was what he wanted. That would help conceal any small noises he may make, no matter how careful he was. The lowering sun cast his shadow behind him.

It was time to take a risk, small as it was. All indicators pointed to an empty dwelling. He approached as cautiously as a gecko emerging from a log. Contented that he was alone, he easily gained entry as the door was not locked. Stepping inside, he looked around, taking in things he'd not seen in decades. A table, chairs, enamel mugs and all the paraphernalia that made a house a home. The aroma of the hut stirred distant memories. There was another scent. It was one of decay. Moving into an adjoining room, he stopped in his tracks. There, reclined against a far wall, were the remains of the occupant.

It was ingrained in him, from boyhood, to show respect.

He offered a fractured prayer to a forgotten God for the repose of the dead man's soul.

Turning to survey the room, he stopped in horror as he caught, for the first time since the fire, so long ago now, his reflection. The face in the mirror wasn't him. He was appalled at the horrific scarring, the disfigurement and the transformation from the handsome young man to what he saw as a grotesque caricature of a human being. If he was unrecognisable to himself, he would be unrecognisable to anybody who may have known him previously.

Being a careful man, he was selective about which of the deceased's wardrobe he liberated. The last thing he wanted or needed was to have his attire recognised. He knew that it might never happen, but then again…

It took him no more than twenty minutes to gather what he needed. Amazingly, the moleskin trousers and the two flannel shirts fitted him. He didn't concern himself with boots. His feet were as tough as ironbark. The swag he rolled was more for show than a necessity. There was a rifle and some ammunition, but something inside warned him to leave them where they were.

In the early twilight, dressed for the first time in over twenty years, he set off to a new start, whatever that may be. He left no sign of his brief incursion into the house. He left no tracks leading to or from the building. It was many miles and two days later that he discarded his aboriginal garb. Little by little, he pulled apart the woven skirt he wore. Little by little, strands of grass found themselves in branches of trees, under rocks or floating in a stream. The belt of hair was unravelled and put to the wind and blown over a cliff.

Back in the archive room of the Word, Shrimp and Milt continued to scan the pages of Widenbridge's past, looking for clues to the mysterious Kelly Daniels.

Rubbing tiring eyes under a naked and inadequate forty-five-watt electric bulb, suspended by fraying flex, Dan reached over and tapped Milt on the forearm.

"Wait a tick, Milt," Dan said. "Can you go back to the obituary? It wasn't much but it may just reveal something."

Searching through sheets of microfiche, Milt found the two- line death notice. 'Daniels - Kelly, died October 12th. He passed away on the wharf boards where he was employed for more than thirty years.'

"That's it, mate," said Shrimp with a hint of excitement. "He worked on the loading docks. We need to search the records of the old steamboat company." Shrimp read the obituary again; something about it didn't quite ring true.

The town noises were heard before the town was seen. Trepidation permeated his being as he approached the town. He didn't know where he was or what colony he was in. What he didn't know was that there were no colonies anymore. Australia was a new nation. Just.

"Ya look lost, cobber," came a voice from behind. "And as out of place as a bishop in a brothel."

Turning, he faced the speaker. The look on the man's face betrayed his horror at what he saw before him, although his speech displayed nothing but kindness and concern. "Strewth, have you been in the wars or what?"

"Wars?"

"Were you fighting the Boer?" the kind voice asked.

The non-committal grunted reply was mistaken for

confirmation of the man's time in conflict in faraway South Africa not too many years before. It was a mistake that was never to be rectified or clarified.

"I saw many horrid things on the battlefield, friend. I know the price and suffering you and your kind went through. Come with me. Have you eaten? Do you have somewhere to sleep? Are you looking for work, by chance?"

Just another grunt was the reply to the questioning.

Walking along Kurrajong Street, the pair certainly made a sight and a cause for comment. Young boys, dared by their mates, ran up to get a close look at the stranger with hardly any hair, a stooped posture and a slight limp. One or two women who saw him covered their eyes and mouths at the horror they witnessed. Still the Reverend Norman Kirkwood led the stranger all the way to his manse. Most of the Reverend's questions were either answered with a grunt or not answered at all.

After accepting the offer of a bath, the stranger sat down to a bowl of soup and some bread and dripping. He devoured the meal slowly, unaccustomed to food that wasn't alive an hour or two before being eaten.

One thing that the stranger did give forth, eventually, was his name. "I need to be able to call you something, friend," the preacher kindly spoke. "What would you be known as in parts where you are from?"

"Kelly is me name, Kelly Daniels," the voice was strained and weary. "Beg ya - pardon me," he said as he raced outside to regurgitate the food that was foreign to his system.

A BENEVOLENT SUN warmed the day. Vegetation was scarcely moved moved by a timid zephyr. Bees and other insects busied themselves with nectar and pollinating duties associated with the plethora of spring flowers. The days were pleasant and the nights were still a touch cool.

Somewhere in the range far to the east, rain had fallen as recently as twelve to fifteen days earlier. It was a significant series of falls that only now was swelling the Wombadgalong River as it slothfully meandered through Widenbridge and beyond. A rise in the river always triggered something in the native fish to bite. It may even have been the springtime that turned the fish into mating mode and food fuelled their procreational activities. Shrimp, being wise to the habits of fish, was there to take advantage of any feeding frenzy that may be happening in the waters by Mullen's Flat.

"I thought I'd find you here," Milt said as he approached Shrimp.

"As perfect conditions as one can expect…. hang on, here we go Milt." The rod in Shrimp's hands bent almost double and line peeled from the reel as a decent sized fish attacked the lure that was proving quite successful. "Will ya grab that net and get it in behind this bloke, please, Milt? Thanks."

"Wow! I'd not believe it if I'd not seen it. That's an absolute rip- snorter. What a cracker!" Milt de Grey was more excited about the fish than the man who caught it.

As Shrimp carefully dispatched the fish into eternal oblivion and started the cleaning and filleting procedures, he invited Milt to a dinner of fish, peas, and mashed potatoes.

"Sounds good to me, mate. I'll bring a few cold ones and a bottle of red."

"Gees Milt," Dan laughed, "if Maggie was still with us, she'd brand you a culinary clown. Fair dinkum, she would shake her head in mock horror, click her tongue, give you that sweet stare of hers before berating you and then educating you that with fish 'One delicately consumes a slightly chilled, but not overly cold Chardonnay or Riesling' before walking away, shaking her head from side to side while muttering something about men with no culture. Red would be just perfect, old mate."

They both laughed.

"What caused you to track me down on such a glorious morning?"

"I've had communication with a company that is about the fourth reincarnation of the old West Rivers Steamboat Transport. They searched their files for me and the letter says that Kelly Daniels started on the loading and storing teams back in 1901. He stayed with them until his death in 1937. Evidently, he camped in one of the wool sheds, rent free, as a mark of respect to his war service. 1901, too early for the big show in Europe that kicked-off when Ferdi was shot, so it must have been South Africa."

REVEREND KIRKWOOD WAS a much-respected man in Widenbridge. He was not without influence. His being a man of the cloth extended way beyond Sunday sermons. He lived a strong Christian ethic, practising what he preached and more. He never pushed the stranger about his past. Many men wouldn't speak of their time in conflict; best left alone. While he was more than happy to house and feed the man who wandered lost into Widenbridge, Reverend Norman Kirkwood knew that a man must have his dignity. Dignity was born of self-respect, self-reliance, independence, and money. Not a fortune, but enough to live on would suffice.

It was after his Sunday service that the preacher took aside Herb Watson, the Chairman of West Rivers Steamboat Transport. The situation was solemnly discussed and arrangements made. The next day, Kelly Daniels began working on the jetty. He helped with the loading and unloading of the small paddlers that worked the smaller rivers that fed the inland arterial waterways. He worked unloading bales of wool, bags of wheat, storing them until the boats were ready to be loaded when they could get through.

Part of the negotiation between the reverend and Mr. Watson was accommodation. Daniels could domicile in a far corner of a storage shed, rent free, as long as he filled the responsibilities of a watchman.

Kelly Daniels kept to himself. He didn't drink with the men. He didn't associate with women. He was a loner. The people of Widenbridge were content to let him be. He worked hard and was more than happy with his own company and thoughts.

The Reverend Norman Kirkwood would call on him from time to time. Conversation was always strained and at times one-sided with the minister, asking the questions and presuming the answers. He gave up attempting to get Kelly Daniels to one of his services and after a while, his visits to the wool shed grew fewer and fewer.

Shrimp and Milt had spent many, many months trying to piece together the mystery of Kelly Daniels. Anybody who may have known anything about him was either dead or no longer in the area.

Records from the West Rivers Steamboat Transport were patchy. Efforts to find military records ran into dead-ends. Shrimp even asked for favours from the police station where he once worked as a detective. All that provided was that

Kelly Daniels was instrumental in saving a little girl from drowning during the flood of 1929.

"I'm surprised that wasn't mentioned in the archives we examined," Shrimp said.

"Ahh! The Word was housed along Loading Street back then and it was well and truly inundated back in the '29 flood. Lots of information floated west," Milt replied, offering a little more of the history of Widenbridge.

To both retired detective Dan Nolan and retired journalist Milton de Grey, the mystery of the man buried in the Widenbridge cemetery was destined to remain just that, a mystery!

At the age of seventy-six years, fifty-seven of them looking over his shoulder since escaping the fire, Kelly Daniels sat on the jetty boards that he'd work on since arriving in Widenbridge in 1901. That was the year Australia became a nation. Even before becoming a nation, Australia already had heroes, villains and some of whom had achieved the status of legend.

Those who knew of Kelly Daniels knew not of the legend to which he belonged, the folklore which he had helped create. He himself knew not of the extent of that legend.

The man with the scars born of a fire long ago, scars that were the result of a conflict, not of a faraway war that others believed scarred him, rested his tired self against a bollard. The pain radiating from the centre of his chest intensified. Breathing became near impossible.

He didn't hear the waters of the Wombadgalong River licking the banks. He didn't hear the dogs barking as they prowled aimlessly through the back streets of Widenbridge, or the sound of the evening train as it built up steam to leave the station. His pain and his memories had taken him back to June 28th, 1880. He could hear the panic inside the engulfed establishment as the flames licked closer. He could hear the ricocheting bullets, one of which penetrated his left shoulder. He could hear the cry from his mate Steve as the body of their brother-in-arms, Joe, fell at their feet.

Kelly Daniels, as the people of Widenbridge knew him, was preparing to exhale his terminal breath, alone. He did not fear the end. He welcomed what was happening to him as his heart prepared for its strangled, final beat.

Had anybody been on the jetty that Tuesday night, they would have seen his weakened eyes brighten and heard the dying man whisper, "I see ya Joe, you too, Stevie boy. And Ned, I'm coming home. Tell the Ma and Katie, the last of the Kelly gang is on his way."

POSTSCRIPT

THE INFAMOUS KELLY GANG, Ned Kelly, Dan Kelly, Steve Hart and Joe Byrne, which terrorised their way across the colonies of Victoria and parts of New South Wales in the latter half of the 1800s, was taken out of circulation by the police at the Siege of Glenrowan, Victoria, on June 28th 1880. It was believed that all except Ned Kelly, the gang leader, were killed either by gunfire or the blaze that destroyed the Glenrowan Hotel.

Ned Kelly was wounded by the constabulary, captured, sent to Melbourne, tried and found guilty of his crimes. He was subsequently hanged in Old Melbourne Gaol on November 11th, 1880.

There were, sometime later, rumours that 19-year-old Dan Kelly escaped. Some stories had him living in and around Brisbane. A man claiming to be Dan Kelly presented himself to the press of the day and the newspapers ran stories that this person was, possibly, the outlaw Dan Kelly.

This story is a fictional alternative to Dan Kelly's alleged escape from Glenrowan.